OFFERINGS FROM A RUST BELT JOCKEY

OFFERINGS FROM A RUST BELT JOCKEY

Andy Plattner

5220 Dexter Ann Arbor Rd.
Ann Arbor, MI 48103
www.dzancbooks.org

The characters and events in this book are fictitious. Any similarity to real persons, living or dead, is coincidental and not intended by the author.

Designed by Steven Seighman

ISBN: 978-1-936873-59-3

First U.S. Edition: September 2014

Printed in the United States of America

10 9 8 7 6 5 4 3 2 1

I.

1.

Carl Arvo knocked on the apartment door of Christine Fleming and then took one step back. The footsteps on the other side of the door stopped and the door didn't open. He supposed that Christine was trying to decide. Perhaps someone else was there with her. Another jockey. Carl didn't mind because what he had to offer her was unique.

Christine opened the door partway and said his name as if she were asking a question.

"Can I talk to you?" he said.

She watched him for a moment. "Will it take long?"

"Might," he said. Carl thought about adding, *Let me say what I'm here to say. You can turn me down and I won't bring it up again.* But this was not what he felt. He was certain that after he said what he had to say, he wouldn't be going away anytime soon.

She wore a thin, light-blue robe with "Bienville House, New Orleans" written in cursive above the left breast. She was almost six feet tall. He supposed she was doing simple math right now, just trying to figure out the quickest way to rid herself of him.

Carl wore a down jacket and stepped forward with his hands in the pockets of his jeans. Inside her apartment, he peeled away the jacket, revealing a brown western-style shirt with white stitching. He had purchased it the day before in Normandy's Department Store on the east end of Cleveland, in the young-teens' section. Carl went to the closest dressing room to try it on. The shirt was tight through the arms but the silver-haired saleswoman said he looked a bit like a young Jason Robards and Carl paid for the shirt in cash.

Christine sat on the loveseat in her small living room and Carl brought over an oval-backed chair made of clear plastic from the kitchen table and sat a few feet from her. The apartment had hardwood floors, aqua-painted walls and three windows that faced to the north. At this time of day, early afternoon, the sun provided a gauzy light. Carl crossed his legs, set an ankle atop a knee. Christine was an owlish, intelligent-looking, slender woman. Her large gray-brown eyes were a bit close together. Her face was heavily freckled and her thick black hair went past her shoulders. She frequently looked quite bewildered. Right now she appeared to be exhausted.

Carl said, "I want to live here this spring and summer with you. Right here in number 206 at Singing Bridge Apartments." His eyes glanced about the room. "For the entire meeting at Summit Park, March through Labor Day. I've been thinking about this for some time, Christine. Now, I want you to hear me out. You know how I finished up at the Randall meet last fall. I got a little hot there. I finished in the riders' standings. Top ten. Well, yes, bottom of the top ten. By the end of the meet, a few trainers asked if I was going to be at Summit this spring. They want to use me. I've been working out horses, and I think I'm about to have the best meeting of my entire life." Carl looked to the windows for a time. "I'm forty-five years old. I can't explain it, though. Why it is happening. But I feel great. After Christmas, I didn't go to ride in West Virginia or Cincinnati. I stayed in town here. I've been going to a gym—L.A. Fitness." He was looking in her direction again.

"No," she said. "Not interested."

"Don't I look like I'm in shape?"

Christine did not respond.

Carl swallowed. "I'm not in love with you," he said. "If you're worried about that. But here is what I've been thinking: I am about to have a good spring and summer. It feels as if luck has blown in my direction from nowhere. I am going to be busy riding horses and I think I'm going to win my fair share of races. I know that much. And what I have decided is that I don't want to spend this time alone. I chased you around a little last fall. I'm glad I did. I like you. I know you like the races, and I know you like to win money at the races."

"My ex-husband gambled away everything," she said. "Everyone knows that."

"Sure," he said. "Last fall, you and I had some laughs. I did. But, anyway, I decided that I don't want to spend this good season by myself. I have two ex-wives. I have three children. My kids are too big to ride, thank God. They don't like me. I am an odd thing in their lives. *My father, the jockey.* You see? I thought about them, though. I have a son. Teddy is his name. He's a sales rep, lives in Camden, New Jersey. Smooth talker, twenty-five, just a few years younger than you. I thought about calling him—letting him stay up here, seeing me win, making some profits on it. That kind of thing would appeal to him. He could see that my life is not all bush league. He accused me of that once, though he was a teenager when he did. I forgave him, obviously.

"I thought about my daughters, who I left when they were only children. I thought a lot about my wives. This winter, I did all of my usual Christmas calls, listened to the sound of their voices as they told me about their New Year's resolutions. I guess, Christine, I was really more than anything just thinking about proving to someone who thought they knew me that I was a winner. I understand I haven't lived an incredible life. This spring, I thought that I just might want someone in my family to see me doing well, see it up close. Everyone wants this, right? When they think about me later on, they could remember this spring and summer, see? They could say that was the year the old man was really hitting the bull's-eye. I thought about all of this for a while. I decided that I don't care anything about it. I thought, you know, I am about to have a really good season at a little racetrack in Cleveland. That's what it is going to be and that is all it is going to be. I'm going to leave the past where it belongs. You are the person I thought of. You are the one I wanted to talk to about it."

In a while, she said, "I don't know you very well."

Carl had surprised her, he could tell this much. He opened his hands when he said, "I just told you everything." He added, "Of course, I would pay half the rent, half the utilities."

Christine dipped her head. "What about sleeping arrangements, Carl?"

"I have slept in your bed before," he said.

She held up two fingers.

"I don't care what the sleeping arrangements are." He inhaled. "I want to hang around with you."

"Why don't you ask me to live with you in your place?"

"I'm tired of my place. I'm just starting to understand how much."

There was a noise in the alley, someone tossing a bag full of bottles into the dumpster. "Sounds like love," she said.

"It's not love," he said. He turned a palm upward. "If I was in love with you, Christine, I would just say that. I would say, 'I am in love with you, Christine.' I'm at a good time in my life. It's going to continue."

"I have to go to work in a little while. What do you mean by winning money at the races?"

"What happened last fall?" he said.

"You liked a horse you rode," she said. "You told me to bet on it. And it won. You spent the night here after this happened. My guess there is that you thought I was a whore."

"Nope."

"I slept with you another time just to prove I wasn't," she said. "That's all."

"You told me that, too," he said.

"Guys at the bar give me grief about my jockey thing," she said. "They say I'm afraid of a full-sized man."

Carl understood that she was testing him and that this was not a bad sign. "What do you care?"

"How do you know you are going to have a good spring?" she said. "How does one in your line of work determine this? Anyway, aren't you as a jockey always supposed to be full of bravado?"

You must have heard that from someone else, he thought, but there wasn't much point in saying it. "You remember that horse I gave you last fall?" he said.

"Big Zip," she said. "You won three races on him, Carl. I remember."

"Big Zip is evidence," Carl said.

"Evidence of?"

"Good things," he said. "That horse was just a bolt from the clouds last October. I got named to ride him the first time because Perry Furlo busted his ankle the race before. Some trainer from Indiana brought in Big Zip. He had never heard of me. He needed a rider and the stewards told him I'd try my best. That I'm not afraid of anything. The horse was crazy, you know? But it ran for me like we'd just done a smash-and-grab from the devil himself. I did win three in a row on it. Even went to Chicago to ride Big Zip in the Michigan Avenue Handicap. I invited you. Remember that?"

"That was like this," she said. "You were all caught up in something."

"We finished third there," Carl said. "A close third. Horse was sold the day after. I haven't seen it since. The new owner took Big Zip to California."

"So?"

"I was caught up in the moment then. I wanted to win the Michigan Avenue 'Cap and then take you to the Drake Hotel afterward. We should've won that race, too. I found out something about how to ride the horse too late."

"I would have lost a whole weekend of tips."

"I know, I know."

"Big Zip put you on a positive streak. I remember that. You were just carried away."

"What happened after that, Christine? After I rode that horse so well in Chicago?"

White light streamed in through the windows now. Beyond the apartment building across the alley the sky was a frothy green color. She looked to Carl again. "You began to ride more winners here," she said. "And you didn't give a single one to me, either."

Carl smiled. He wanted to make a joke but could not come up with one. "I kept my mouth shut," he said. "That is true. Honestly, I just wanted to concentrate. I began to wonder, is this my prime, at last? Something like that. Hell, I just wanted to finish the meet on a high note. I did, too. Trainers were happy with me. A lot of them promised me business for the spring. They opened the track for training last week. I've been getting on a lot of live horses, Christine."

"Moving in with me will break your concentration." Her voice sounded empty. "I have been known to have that effect on men."

"I can concentrate," he said. "I want to do more than that." Carl leaned forward in his chair. "I didn't expect you to have an answer for me today. All I ask is that you think about it."

"I am going to tell you it's not the best idea I've ever heard, Carl," she said. "That can be today or it can be tomorrow."

"You liked being with me when we were together last fall," he said. "I felt that." She didn't respond. "What I'm proposing is not a business arrangement. We're two people who simply like one another. I will admit that I might like you more. I will be your friend. And I want to make you money."

"You can promise that?" she said.

"No promises," he said. "But, I am going to be good this spring and I want to share it with somebody."

A silence went on for a minute, then another. He tried to think of what he could add. Before he figured out anything else, she said, "I'll call you in a couple of days. Okay? That's the best answer I can give."

He nodded at this. He wished for more. He felt certain about all that he had already said to her. He stood. All he could think of to say then was "Thank you."

Carl lived in a rent-by-the-week apartment on Thurston Avenue in Cleveland Heights, down the street from an abandoned three-story manufacturing plant with busted windows and ground-level graffiti that covered half a city block. There they had made spaghetti and ravioli in one-person servings zipped up in tin cans. HiLo Foods had pulled out of Cleveland in the late seventies and they'd left town fast. The assembly line had stayed in place. Conveyor belts, ominous vats, intestines of metal tubing—these rusted, decaying artifacts still visible through the smashed-out windows of the building all these years later. Carl could get by with the rent on Thurston Avenue, and the old factory comforted him. He had been raised in Burgundy, West Virginia, a steel-mill town gasping for life. Men were losing their jobs, but no one seemed to know what to do about it. They'd never known anything but their jobs, and these jobs were all they wanted to know. His size wouldn't prevent him from working in the mill. But he saw his unusual height as a way out of whatever life was going to be left in Burgundy. He had quit high school to work at a horse barn at old Waterford Park, just a few miles to the north of his hometown. He had been working at one racetrack or another ever since.

After he made his proposal to Christine, Carl spent the evening at his wobbly-legged kitchen table. He owned a laptop, something he'd bought to celebrate his victory aboard a 36–1 bomb in the Samuel Handicap at Beulah Park. For a couple of weeks, Carl's business had experienced a positive bump. Then he was back to riding in one or two races a day on horses who had little chance of winning.

Still, Carl was glad to have the computer as evidence of his positive outlook. He regularly visited websites featuring daily news about horse racing. He became more curious about the whereabouts of old acquaintances or horses he'd previously won on. If he saw the horse was on a losing streak now, Carl might sift through his address book and email the trainer: *Look, I won on it once, I can do it again.* A trainer believed he or she, not some no-name rider, was the one who had the key to a horse. It was a long shot that a trainer would pay any attention, but Carl kept trying anyway. He never wanted to stop trying. Trainers declined his offers. Sometimes they did this ever so tactfully. On the whole, more than a few people seemed to understand how important riding was to him.

Carl kept two email addresses—one for his personal life and one for his business. He had the email addresses of his ex-wives and his children. He was Facebook friends with them all and he received a fairly steady stream of friend requests from racetrackers he knew. Some were from people he hadn't spoken to in a decade or more. Brian Holstead, whom Carl had ridden against in Erie for one largely forgettable year, announced that he had just been released from the Parchman State Prison in Joplin, Missouri, after spending sixteen years there for a drug-dealing conviction. Tammy Beck, a one-time groom for Smiley Adams, currently worked on a community farm in Sandsill, Oregon. Aja Banks, an exercise rider he'd known in Michigan, had a track pony fall on her a few years back and now walked around with the aid of two metal canes. For his personal Facebook info, Carl supplied the basics but rarely provided updates like *Going out with friends tonight* or *Riding a bunch of winners this afternoon.* Facebook made him think of the ancient TV show *This Is Your Life.* He'd led the life he was supposed to, yet most everything had passed him by. He was interested in the photos posted by his family and friends. He looked at some of the photos for a very long time. He'd study photos of the smiling people, the way the sunlight played on their faces, the ways in which they were aging. Even though people were smiling in them, the photos reminded Carl there were not many great options in this life. He looked over the photos and felt relieved.

Carl opened a spreadsheet on his laptop. A small, spiral-bound notebook sat alongside the computer. He recorded the names of the horses he worked out, as well as particular commitments he'd made for working out horses tomorrow and the days beyond. He wore reading glasses. Carl didn't like to turn down business, but he also didn't want to promise to be at a certain barn at a certain time and then discover he already had a previous engagement. He kept most of this in his head, but the spreadsheet cemented everything. It helped when it was time to make out his bills. Many trainers liked to get a hard copies of their bills because it helped them keep their books straight, too. Others were less worried about it. Carl didn't mind working horses for fly-by-night outfits. If anything, this sharpened his skills for collecting what he was owed.

The sheet showed no conflicts in his schedule for tomorrow morning. He printed it out, looked it over one more time. He checked his cell phone for messages. He had three, though none were from Christine. Two messages were from trainers reminding Carl about workout promises he had made for later in the week, and Carl made notations on his spreadsheet immediately. The last message was from a jockey agent Carl knew, Ilya Kamanakov.

"Hello there, Cahlavo, this is Ilya calling you again. I want to talk with you, Cahl. I want to take on your book for the meet. If you want, I can double your business. I can get you on as many good horses as you would like. Call me."

Carl liked how Ilya turned his name into one word. *Cahlavo* sounded like an exotic locale—one that purposeful young couples rode in Jeeps for hours just to get a glimpse of. Ilya was close to Christine's age, but he already knew better than to try and sound like he understood something a jockey did not. Ilya was a bright kid, definitely on the way up. His family was from the Ukraine and they'd come to Pittsburgh when he was eight years old. Ilya's parents worked for a company that manufactured rubber dishes, but Ilya wasn't going to settle for that.

Carl laid his phone on the table, sat back in his chair. It had been at least a half-dozen years since he'd had an agent. Carl would win some races, gain the attention of an agent, and the agent parlayed the wins into more rides. When Carl went into a slump—and this always happened, Carl always went into inexplicable funks—the agent would drop him. Over time he had learned to handle every aspect of his business himself. He knew that if he stepped back and looked at his career on the whole, it could be said that as a jockey, he didn't make for much of a businessman. But he was still a jockey. Sometimes, this seemed like the only thing that actually mattered.

Ilya would continue to call him, Carl understood this, because that was what an agent did. Carl tried to imagine he was living with Christine but didn't have this paperwork to tend to. Then he imagined living here, in this by-the-week apartment, without the paperwork. He lifted his cell phone from the table, found Ilya's number. Ilya answered on the second ring and said, "Look who, the greatest jockey in America today."

"Hello, Ilya. I am returning your call."

"I have a pen in my hand and I want to carry it over to you right now. Sign on the line, my man."

Carl waited a moment. He liked Ilya's approach. "What are you offering?" and then he wondered if he shouldn't have called Ilya after Christine made her decision.

"The moon," he said. "In return, I get fifteen percent of all purses. Twenty percent on all stakes races."

"We aren't going to be riding in any stakes races up here."

"I might find you some out-of-town work. Maybe we'll find another horse like Beeg Zip."

"That would be something," Carl said.

"I looked over the barn lists and the first condition book. I saw what you were on at the end of last meet. These trainers, they spot a little something in you. I can increase your money by what, forty percent?"

"Your message said you could double my business."

"I want you to call me back."

"What about communication between you and me?"

"I speak perfect," Ilya said.

"No," Carl said. "I mean, we would have to talk every day, I guess."

"Of course," Ilya said. "I know you don't need help with your eating. But there might be something you see, a horse you would like to ride. A horse you want to stay away from. Anything."

"Right," Carl said. "I'll tell you what. I really don't like making big plans, you know? So, we would have to figure out that part of it. Shit, I don't want to sit down every day and talk to you about what we are going to do about all these cheap horses around here. But I'll sign with you. A two-year contract. Two years, thick and thin." He held off from saying *my man.*

"I was thinking about till Fourth of July," Ilya said. "Then we see where we are."

"Two years," Carl said.

"Suppose you get hurt?"

"If I get hurt, you have to bring me the newspaper every day and do the goddamn dishes in my sink."

"You don't want an increase in your money right now, Cahl?"

Carl exhaled, felt his shoulders relax. Ilya's was not a bad offer at all. Carl would not get one like this every day. "Can I call you if it turns out I can't handle what I have here?" He laughed a bit, hoping Ilya might.

"I need a rider, Carl. The meet starts next week. Rules say I can have one journeyman, one apprentice."

"Who's the apprentice?"

"Boy from Juárez. Rafael Barrero."

"Yeah, I rode against him once or twice last fall. Might've thumped into him once. Didn't soak himself."

"He's not afraid of anything."

"Yet," Carl said.

Ilya laughed at this. "Yes."

"Does Darryl McFadden have an agent?"

"He is with Shelly Fronk."

"Look," Carl said. "I just can't say yes right now, Ilya. I'm trying to get things a certain way. Trying to keep the number of people in my life to a minimum. I guess that's what it is."

"I have to look for other riders."

"I understand," Carl said. "If you don't hear from me in the next twenty-four hours..."

"I am supposed to talk with Guillermo Milord tonight," Ilya said.

Milord was washed up, had completely lost his nerve. Was Ilya trying to make Carl feel sorry for him? Carl already had a sinking feeling, though. Whether he went with Ilya or not, he would be missing something. "I am going to handle my own stuff," Carl said. "Thanks."

Ilya said, "Good luck then, Cahl. Bye."

2.

The following morning, Carl arrived at the Summit Park backstretch at five thirty a.m. and his first mount of the morning was one of his favorite horses on the grounds, a seven-year-old gelding named A Letter to Harry. The sky was still cloaked in late-night purple as Carl worked the horse over a heavy track and galloped him out another quarter of a mile. The horse's trainer had asked for a four-furlong work in forty-eight seconds, but they had gone much slower than that, fifty-one or even fifty-two. The horse felt good under Carl, but at this age it wasn't going to go any faster. Following the workout, Carl rode the horse at a walk along the outside rail of the homestretch, headed in the opposite direction of horses striding out for the finish line. Carl sat peacefully in the saddle. The cell phone inside Carl's down vest began to vibrate. He held the reins in his left hand and used his right to unzip his pocket. He held the phone so he could see the number.

"Yes?"

"I'm here," Christine said.

Carl turned in the direction of the glassed-in grandstand. There were no lights on inside, no human silhouettes on the asphalt apron between the grandstand and the racing oval. Two horses working side by side churned their way down the homestretch, and from behind Carl, coming down the outside rail, a rider and horse neared. They moved on by. A gruff voice, a female's, said, "Off the road, you old bitch!" Carl thought he knew the voice—Becky Hiltz—and what she was saying was to get off the phone. Early morning hours were busy at the track, schedules getting turned upside down on a regular basis. You needed to check your calls, but not on horseback—not even if you were on a reliable creature like A Letter to Harry.

"I don't see you," Carl said.

"I am waiting for you in the track kitchen," she said. "Right now."

"I'll be right there." Carl closed the phone, dropped it into his pocket. He wanted to touch his heels to the horse's ribs, get him going faster, but this horse liked being on the track. A Letter to Harry was not a fast horse, but he was something of an unusual one. Carl leaned forward, said, "Walk faster. One time, for me." He was not going to do anything more than plead. There were certain horses that earned this type of treatment. Horses that liked their jobs and were at home on the track. These were the horses that made Carl feel even better about his own work, and this was the most important thing, even more than what any woman could do for him.

When he was young, Carl hadn't dreamed of being a jockey. He couldn't remember much of that time now. All he knew was that he'd wanted to leave his hometown forever. He knew that and could still feel that part of his youth: the feeling that as long as he got away, whatever was going to happen could happen. He'd been sixteen years old and in the middle of his sophomore year of high school when he dropped out to work at Waterford Park with a former Marine Corps staff sergeant and recovering alcoholic, a trainer named Sherman Ingram. Carl spent his first year at the track shoveling out stalls—ten a day—and walking hots. He slept in a tackroom at the barn and lost his virginity there to a big, forty-one-year-old assistant trainer, Beverly Motion. He hung around with career grooms and card players and two-dollar gamblers, and he began to learn what he needed to know. Ingram had an old pony named Lips that he let Carl ride around the barn area after training hours. By the time Carl began exercising horses on the track, he'd felt the rest of his life was more or less laid out for him. Early in his riding career, Carl had loved horses—but his winning, or lack thereof, began to color his love in the time that followed. But he understood they had given him control, some say in his own life. By his early twenties, Carl's relationship with horses had become less than glorious. Already a struggling journeyman rider changed by consistent losing, he had to fight with too many horses to get them to run their best. In the mornings, a horse would try to buck him from its back or run off while he battled to rein it in. These were rebellious acts and he became more aggressive with his use of the whip. A horse no longer represented freedom, it reflected a misguided ambition. He'd heard that horses were not such rogues on the major circuits in New York and Miami, that getting on the back of a runner there was like test-driving a Porsche. After he divorced his first wife, Kelly, Carl decided to try his luck on the big circuit and he spent one winter and spring galloping horses in Miami. He freelanced, went from barn to barn each morning looking for work. Towards the end of the meeting at Tropical

Park, a trainer promised him mounts on a couple of horses. The horses didn't belong in the majors and they were badly outrun in their races. The end of spring saw Carl demoralized and flat broke. The track chaplain gave him bus fare, and like that he was off to Pennsylvania to try and build his business at Penn National in Harrisburg. He met a woman at a grocery store, Alycia Pettit. He eventually married her. He began to win races again. Carl felt his relationship with horses shifting at Penn National. Once in a while, a horse and Carl Arvo had the same thing in mind: victory. All that mattered, all he knew for certain, was that riding made him brave. Riding gave him a manageable life. He knew things about the world because of his work. Without it, he might have been scared of everything. He told himself that he was fortunate. It was good to be alive and be a part of something. What he had learned was that it didn't matter where this happened to be.

When Carl returned A Letter to Harry to the barn, he dismounted in an expedient way, then disconnected the overgirth and the girth and pulled away the saddle. Carl handed the big tangle of equipment over to the groom and said, "Tell the boss this is the smartest horse I've ever been on."

The groom was a young guy with bushy hair, and in the darkness this was all Carl could really see. "Okee dokee," he said.

A horse had already been saddled up for him at Denny Roster's barn. Carl walked over, nodded to Denny and a man in a tweed cap and hunting jacket and said, "Look, something has come up and I have to take care of it right now. I'll get on two horses for you tomorrow, free of charge." Carl put out his hand to shake with Denny. "Yes? It's personal."

"You all right?" Denny said, shaking Carl's hand.

"Fine," Carl said. "Thank you." He nodded again to both men and began walking in the direction of the track kitchen. He supposed they watched him. *Imagine that little prick.* Denny was a man who trained a string of two dozen horses. He was used to making a hundred decisions every morning, and he would have instantly decided whether to use Carl tomorrow. The best trainer made educated guesses about how to find the best in his horses. The unpredictability of human lives could not be part of this equation. Anyone who failed to understand this—or even forgot it momentarily—might not be welcome for long at any barn.

Carl did not turn back. He had made a mistake, an unusual one for a man of his years and experience, but Denny might cut him some slack. These years of experience should this one time count for something.

Carl supposed that if he had hired him, Ilya would be over at Denny's barn right now, smoothing things over, rearranging schedules, making promises. Carl tried to imagine a life with a lawyer, an accountant, a personal trainer, agents—he wouldn't have to think about a thing. He imagined himself in a dark blue robe, seated out on a lounge near a crystal clear swimming pool. He might get into philanthropy, create something. An Unknown Jockeys Foundation.

A six-foot-high stretch of hurricane fence separated the track kitchen from the barn area and a security guard with long white hair—a tall man perched high on his stool—watched over the one spot where the fence sections were disconnected. He sat with his arms crossed and he nodded in a solemn way as Carl walked through the opening. Carl strolled to the kitchen and pulled open a glass door. Inside, he took in the familiar aromatic combination of bacon/coffee/manure/hay/Absorbine. Christine sat at one end of a cafeteria table. Four dark-haired men in deep gray jumpsuits occupied the other half of it. These men worked in janitorial, or were with track maintenance. At the far end of the room one of the pool tables sat empty and the game at the other apparently had been abandoned. Pool balls and two sticks were left on the felt. Two grooms, caught slacking by a boss. One of the jumpsuit men talked to Christine as Carl approached and Christine began to nod to her head. A cantaloupe rind along with a twice-bitten biscuit sat on the plate in front of her.

He took the seat across from her, noticed the glassiness of her eyes. She wore a long-sleeve t-shirt with a gray sweater vest over it. Her hair was tied in a ponytail behind her head. "Carl," she said, "I am pretty tired of losing." She held her hands flat on the table. The track workers at Carl and Christine's table all smoked cigarettes. "It's bright in here," she said. Carl started to speak, but Christine continued, "I think you're a nice man," she said. "I like it that you are feeling so optimistic about your future." Her eyes, pink at the edges, went to his. He did not think she had been crying. "I would like to make some money," she said. "Do you really think I can?"

"Yes," he said.

"I've seen a lot of riders walk in and out of here this morning. It's different. My ex-husband is a gambler."

"You said that," he said.

"He's still around," she said. "Trying to stay in the picture. Have you met him?"

"Maybe at the bar," Carl said. "Tall guy. Blond hair. You didn't introduce him or anything like that."

"How do you know it was my ex?"

"He looked at you different," Carl said. "I thought he was somebody to you. Let's put it that way."

She said, "You have exes call you at all hours?"

"No."

"I see," she said. "Well, my ex is the one who started taking me to the racetrack. We had our honeymoon in New Orleans, went to the Fair Grounds every day." *I always wanted to ride there.* Carl could have said this. He thought, *Probably would have starved.* "When we moved up here, he wanted to live close to the track. So that's how I wound up taking the job at the Seven Seas. All he did, all he does, is lose. Stripped bare our bank accounts." Carl looked to the men seated at the other half of the table and the eyebrows on one of them went up. Christine said, "After he left, I started to make friends with some of the riders. When you know the right people, horse racing is not as difficult to figure out, is it, Carl?"

"It's still pretty difficult," he said.

"Yeah, well," she said.

Carl looked to the table top, the space between them, and then he glanced at Christine again. "I want to live with you," he said. "I think I know what you are doing here."

"Man, maybe you can tell me."

They watched one another. In a quiet way, he said, "You are trying to tell me that you are an angry bitch."

"No." She shook her head slightly, touched her right index finger to the table top. "I am telling you I haven't made up my mind completely as yet. I will soon, though."

He said, "You are telling me that you will not abide a man who makes you unhappy."

Christine looked at her plate. "I guess in so many words that is what I am trying to tell you. Also, there is no way I will agree to six months. Absolutely not."

"Just the Summit meeting," Carl said.

"No."

"Okay. All right."

Carl didn't think he had ever seen her looking quite this way. He wanted to say something to the men listening from the other half of the table. "I will be good to you," Carl said. "You can count on that."

"I'm going back to my apartment now," she said. "Call me this afternoon. We can agree to something." She smiled in a tired-looking manner then. "Something unambitious, okay? Maybe something that might last a day or two."

Carl waved his hand in front of his chest. "I'll take it."

3.

Later that afternoon, during the course of a friendly discussion on the phone, Carl and Christine agreed to a trial run, a test of living together that would, in fact, go on for two and a half days, beginning one week before the Summit meeting began. Carl would arrive on Saturday afternoon at 4 p.m. and stay until Tuesday morning. Whatever she decided after this would be final. There would be no protests from Carl—not if he ever wanted to be friends with her again.

Christine opened the door for him on Saturday afternoon. She held on to the knob and stood in the opening. More than anything, she looked as if she simply wanted to close the door again. Carl understood that people sometimes looked at him and thought, *This is it? This is what you have to offer?* It appeared as if she might close the door, but she didn't.

"It's a big move," Carl said. "Even though this is just a tryout."

Christine's eyes were on his gym bag and his computer case. He held the handles for both in his left hand. On any day when there was live racing, Carl exercised horses in the mornings, then drove over to the jockeys' quarters, which were adjacent to the Summit Park clubhouse. He showered, had a quick, tiny breakfast—he liked almonds, as many as ten of them—then played ping-pong or five-card draw with some of the other idle jocks. Killed time until the races began. Last summer, he'd spent many useless afternoons in the jocks' quarters, from the first race to the last. Waiting for someone else to get injured or get sick or just beg off his mounts for the day, he became a ping-pong Jedi. Inside the gym bag was a change of clothes, underwear, a *USA Today*, a Scott Turow paperback, a pint of brandy, a jockstrap and five Ace bandages. He always wrapped his elbows and his knees. He could put these bandages on tomorrow morning, while Christine was asleep.

If Christine had been a straight nine-to-fiver, he still would have wanted to be with her this spring. She tended bar and that meant she worked mainly at night. They would be in the apartment together sometimes, but not as much as other couples. Carl felt this to be significant. She was ultimately going to agree to his proposal and after she did, he would find himself alone in her apartment for hours every day. He wanted this. He didn't want to invade her privacy, or try on her underwear while she was away. He just didn't want to be alone and if he had to be he did not want to be solely amongst his own things. He had lived in enough motel rooms, by-the-week apartments. It must have been a relief for Christine to see he had brought along just a gym bag and his computer. He supposed this could've been why she eventually pushed the door back for him.

Carl nodded. "Good afternoon. Thank you," he said. They did not embrace. They did not touch one another. Carl appreciated the oddness of the situation. This was something he had asked for. He thought he should say something else. "I wanted to bring you a bottle of wine," he began. "Or even champagne. I walked through the liquor store a little while ago. But nothing seemed right. I thought, good lord, she works around this stuff every day already."

"Oh, don't worry about it."

"I really don't drink that much," he said. With his free hand, he tapped his midsection. "When he was at the top of his game, Laffit Pincay Jr. ate a leaf of lettuce and a tin of tuna for dinner. You know who that is, right?"

"A jockey."

"That's right," Carl said. "Sure." The wooden floor creaked under the soles of his boots as he shifted his weight. He rubbed at his mouth with his free hand and said, "How's your day going?" He set the computer case on the maroon vinyl loveseat.

"I made space for you, a drawer in my bureau," she said. "That's for the little stuff, socks, underwear. In the closet by the front door there are shelves for winter clothes. You can set up your laptop on the kitchen table."

He thought about making a joke, something to do with a jockey sleeping in a drawer. Carl was his own man, however. Since he had been riding horses he had felt this way. He followed her into the bedroom. Christine owned a cat named Bo, just like the president's dog. He detected a cat-box odor. Carl had been in this bedroom before, but the cat had stayed out of sight. With Christine seated at the foot of the bed, Carl walked across the room and placed the contents of his gym bag into the top drawer. The bureau was made of pine, painted chocolate brown. Probably had come with the apartment or was something she had picked up at a second-hand store.

When the gym bag was empty, he folded it, set it on his things in the drawer. He walked over and sat atop the foot of the bed, not far from her.

He said, "Don't panic, don't let it bother you. I've lived with other tall women. There's always that feeling to start off. Know what I like to do when I think a woman is worried about how much of man I am? Know what I like to show her?"

Christine sat on the edge of the bed with her legs crossed. She held her hands in her lap.

Carl held his arms in her direction. "My hands," he said. He smiled a bit at this. "Look at these. All knobs and stumps. I have broken seven different fingers. And, a thumb. The thumb hurt worse than anything." He flexed it a few times. With each flex, a sound. "Tic, toc, tic, toc," he said. He brought his hands back, then he sat forward on the bed. He felt as if things were going well. "I cracked my pelvis at Penn National. Broke my shoulder at Bowie. This was years ago, however."

She said, "I've been thinking about it. I think you ought to sleep in the bed. There's the loveseat out in the living room. But that's barely big enough for Bo. Even if you are a fetal sleeper. You're not a fetal sleeper are you?"

"Not really."

"That would be weird anyway. You sleep in bed with me. I am trying not to make a lot of rules. I thought about it. I thought about having a lot of rules. It has been my experience that rules simply prolong the inevitable. I think to have a lot of rules for a two-and-a-half-day trial run would be crazy. So the bed is okay. We ought to share that. Just don't come cruising over when I'm asleep."

"We'll be in bed together about two hours a night," he said. "I think it'll be nice for me to wake up and see you there." The honesty of this remark surprised her, he thought. But, then, he had been honest with her all along.

"You don't need an alarm, do you?" she said. "If I remember right."

"No," he said. "I do not." *I have been waking up at four thirty in the morning every morning since Reagan took office.*

Christine said, "I have to be at work in a little while. I wanted to be here to show you around. I really don't keep a lot of food in the fridge. There's a Food Lion down that way, about three blocks. Or the Italian place is over there." She waved her arm over her head. He watched her. She dropped her arm to her side, swallowed. "A tin of tuna?"

"You can squeeze a little lemon in there," he said. He moved an index finger in a circle. "You just have to eat it real slow. You use the taste as the thing, not the amount."

Christine nodded. "Cheap date."

"Well," he said. "It is that."

Christine dressed for work and Carl set up his laptop on the kitchen table. There would be room for a printer, but for now he could do without it. Carl had his schedule for tomorrow morning memorized. He'd spend half of it galloping horses for Denny Roster. He had caught up with Denny, explained things. Carl had said, Right, it was about a woman. But, I like her. Denny had seemed surprised by this. He'd said, Shit, Carl, why didn't you just say that? Carl wanted to square things anyway and Denny said fine, set aside a few hours. Even though Carl had to move other commitments around to do so, he quickly agreed. He would be getting on Denny's worst horses, and following this everything would fine between them.

He found a magazine on the foot-high glass coffee table in the living-room area. He took a place on the loveseat, and turned the pages of the *Metropolis*. The door to the bedroom was closed. The magazine had a subscription tag at the bottom—facing upside down—and he wondered how interested he should try to be in the articles. The content seemed purposeful. Smarter design. More colors and surprising shapes. Ergonomics. Anything to help the environment. Overall, it seemed to be a brainy, energetic embrace of the tomorrow-is-less philosophy. Carl felt whimsical. I will wind up being a man of my time after all, he thought. The magazine featured photographs of a floating house project in Rotterdam, an apartment complex set right onto a canal. Carl thought, I am used to being hungry. I have adapted to this. He tried to make an exact distinction between being hungry and planning for the future. The future, well, it could be nice. It could look promising in a magazine. Being hungry forced your hand. Carl was used to one and he wondered if this would ever change. Christine stepped out from behind the bedroom door. She wore the same jeans, a white blouse and a black sweater vest. Shined boots, a down jacket folded over one arm. Carl stood, held on to the magazine. They nodded to one another and then she stepped toward him. "Here's a key," she said. Things were going nicely. He knew that, and he thought that she knew that.

After Christine left the apartment, Carl walked over to the kitchenette. He had to get on his toes to open the cupboards over the sink. Inside, she had box mixes for creole dishes and small sacks of powdered sugar and cornmeal. On one shelf sat a dark blue plastic batting helmet with a Cleveland Indians logo. It seemed like something from a giveaway day at a baseball game, something she would decide was insignificant when enough time had passed. Inside the refrigerator he found near-empty bottles of teriyaki sauce, ketchup and barbecue sauce, unopened jars of mustard and olive spread, a weary-looking stick of butter. Three cans of Miller beer, a bottle of Washington State chardonnay. Carl touched the back of his hand to the neck of the bottle. He wanted to open it, have a glass, but she might be saving it for something. It could be a valuable vintage. He brought the bottle from the shelf, checked the label. The label had a drawing of a man and a woman on a bicycle built for two. He did not want to have to mark what belonged to her or to him with a Sharpie. Besides, both of their names started with a *C*. He memorized the label, the name of the winery. For the right price, he'd buy five bottles of it at the supermarket, surprise her.

Outside, the wind moved fast and the warmth of the air surprised him. In a way, Carl couldn't believe how well things seemed to be going. He tried to understand if anything could be false about the way he felt. He had good vibes about his riding but he didn't want this to blind him to everything else. If he rode five winners each day for the rest of his life it wouldn't mean he ought to start believing life had all of this meaning to it—"God had made this world and all the jockeys in it." An idea to be filed under wishful thinking, at best. That ship had already sailed for him. Carl regretted not having faith, but he didn't regret it all that much. Other riders did believe and it worked for them. The great Hall of Fame jockey Pat Day, in a gesture of gratitude, used to motion towards heaven with his whip after he won a race. Carl would see this on an ESPN clip and think, a fast horse is better than an invisible God, Pat.

Pat Day found God in a motel room while he watched a sermon from Jerry Falwell. Day had told the story many times and while Carl admired Day's earnestness, he felt the story belittled riders overall. Day described himself as a "sinner," a man in need of salvation. Following his conversion, he became the leading jockey in America; they put him in the Hall of Fame well before he even retired from the game. Day's prime had come when Carl was in his mid-twenties and struggling.

Late one night, after his first wife Kelly had gone to sleep, Carl was watching sermons on cable. He sat on their Rent-a-Center sofa, laid his hands on his knees, turned up his palms. He closed his eyes and he waited. He'd been involved in race-fixing at every track he'd been to. Every time he blinked Kelly was pregnant.

He sat there with his palms turned up and after a time, he understood that God would not be reaching out to him. He didn't want to feel cheated by this.

Kelly took their children and left him and for the year after that, Carl went through a predictable lawless phase. He popped speed, he made promises to any woman who'd listen. He took wild chances during races. He fought with other riders in the jocks' room and once broke his hand after punching a shower head that didn't produce enough hot water. He received a couple of suspensions for reckless riding. The second one lasted for three months, and he wound up bagging groceries during this time. He tried to understand why things weren't working out any better. There ought to be a time when he should stop worrying about it. He worked on this, he stuck other people's groceries into plastic bags, told himself that to go forward he needed to give up on the things holding him back. He needed to not worry about Pat Day. God could stay away. Carl could figure out things for himself.

His suspension served, Carl went back to the track, promised himself not to ask for more than this. In time, he began to win races and when he won he sometimes felt gratified that he didn't have God in his life. He would replay a winning ride over and over in his mind and he would think, I got that on my own. He tried to explain this to his second wife, Alycia, a devout Catholic, and early in their marriage she listened with patience. Once, they sat up in bed together and talked about heaven and hell and he said it didn't matter because both places should be like a Spencer's Gifts store with the multicolored skull-shaped candle holders and the incense and the sex-themed board games. He wanted her to scold him a little, but she just shook her head. She smiled at him and he said, That's all I really need to believe.

Alycia said, The Spencer's part, I didn't know that. Not specifically. The rest I did.

4.

On Sunday afternoon, Carl and Christine sat on clear plastic chairs at her table for two that looked out to the brick apartment building across the alley. Sunlight poured in through the windows. The kitchen table was square, the top made of glass, the legs aluminum, the whole thing on wheels. The coffee pot sat on a folded hand towel. Each of them drank from a white mug. He had gotten home a half an hour earlier. She wore her Bienville House robe. Christine said, "So what's with all the tuna fish in the cupboard? When I started to look for something to eat here, I guessed I was cracking up. How many you got in there?"

"Two dozen."

Christine placed her hand to her forehead. "Man," she said. "All that wine in the fridge, too. Thank almighty God I don't have to go in till six today." She kept her hand to her forehead. "Did I wake you up last night?"

"I felt it when you got into bed," he said. "But that didn't wake me."

"If you felt it, how did it not…all right, I don't care. I mean I care, but I don't." Christine used both of her hands to push back her hair. She leaned forward, set her crossed arms on the table. "So," she said, "tell me about the business part of this."

"Good," Carl said. He nodded. "Glad to."

"Well?"

"Christine," he said. "I've been thinking about something and I guess this is a good a time to talk about it as any."

She said, "You tired of me hanging my underwear on the shower rod?"

"Well."

"Go ahead."

"It has to do with you sleeping with me."

She tilted her chin upward, leaned back. "Oh," she said. "We really are going to talk about something."

Carl flashed a quick smile. He felt patient. "I think you should sleep with me when you want to," he said. "That's going to be the bottom line in all of this."

"I'm going to sleep with you when I want to," she said. "Jesus."

"Maybe I don't need to say anything else about it."

"Is that the way it's been, women screw you when you are winning and leave you alone when you aren't?"

"Some of it has been like that. But not all of it. I don't want you to get mad. But if and when the money starts to roll in, you might think, Hell, I need to give this guy a little something in return."

"So?"

"I am just saying you don't have to."

"Maybe I'll just fuck you when you are losing, turn your world upside down." Her voice was dry. She held her arms against her stomach. "Why are we talking about this? I am going to do whatever I want."

Carl thought for a moment. He held out one hand, palm up. "Let's go to bed right now," he said.

"What?" she said. She turned in the direction of the windows. Sunlight fell across her face and she closed her eyes. She placed the butt of her right palm between her eyes. Slowly, she said, "Right this second, I wouldn't fuck you if you were Tom Brady in a Browns jersey. Let's just talk about business, all right, Carl? That's what I asked you to start with."

"Okay. Look, are you all right?"

"When I got home last night, I found all these bottles of wine in the fridge. Why did you do that?"

"I saw the bottle you had in there. I guess I felt like doing something nice for you."

"I am going to be sick." Before anything else happened, she was. Christine fell forward in her chair and spit on the floor. She sat hunched over in her chair and retched. Carl stood from his chair and went to her side. He reached to keep her hair clear. Christine lurched away from him, ran for the bathroom.

Carl fetched a roll of paper towels from a kitchen cabinet and began tearing away sections. He placed sheets of paper towels atop the mess on the floor. He stood near the mess and his eyes went to the window, the brick apartment building across the alley. The blinds were closed tight against the windows in the apartment across from Christine's. There had been a year when Carl was between wives and riding at Detroit Race Course. That year, he had a small apartment in a four-story building on Dequindre Avenue. He lived on the third floor and the windows faced a third-floor unit in the building across an alley. For a while, a man and a woman, both of whom worked day jobs, shared the place. The man wore a jacket and a tie, the slender woman favored pants suits. They sat across from one another at the dinner table; they gestured as they spoke. Day in, day out, what could there possibly be to say? Carl turned off all of his lights in the evening. The man and the woman fought then. They drank and smoked and for a while they snorted coke.They didn't bother to close the blinds. Carl thought that in their own way they were trying hard, working on their lives like crazy. They wanted everything. He thought, Dry out, just want a little less. He wanted to phone them, offer advice, but of course that would never work. The woman finally stopped coming home. The man lived there by himself for another month.

Then the man did something remarkable. He brought home two cans of black paint, opened one, then the other, and proceeded to toss the contents of both against the walls. The next day, the man was gone. Carl never saw him inside the apartment again. The walls looked like someone had been trying to articulate nothing more than a bad dream. Voyeurism on the whole was a valuable thing to Carl. He felt as if he could watch people in their apartments until the end of time, like everything he needed to know could be discovered if he just paid enough attention. In the days that followed, painters arrived, men in white overalls who stood on ladders and turned the walls light green. Carl watched them work and found himself hoping another couple would move in when the apartment was ready. He was having nothing but bad luck riding that year at DRC. Agents avoided him. The horses he rode were balky, they had issues about trying—they were sore, sour, defeated.

The bathroom door opened and he waited for a second before turning in that direction. Christine said, "I'm so sorry."

"I'll get it." He turned just enough to acknowledge her. Her footsteps grew fainter. The sound of a door opening, then closing. The bedroom. Carl went to the kitchen, took out two plastic grocery sacks. He went to the table and the vomit on the floor. He knelt and began to pick up the soiled paper towels. He spent a few minutes dealing with the warm mess. He tied the used paper towels in one sack and then put the other sack over this. He set it by the front door and went to the bathroom to wash his hands. He dried them on a hand towel, walked to the bedroom door and tapped on it twice.

"Come in."

Christine was stretched out on the bed, her hands pressed down on Bo the cat, who sat on her midsection. "Stay," she said. The orange cat began to wriggle backward, so she lifted her hands, let it go. The cat skittered down to the floor and under the bed. Christine lay with her legs crossed at the ankles. She wore white socks. She folded her hands over her stomach. She said, "You did not have to clean that up. I wish you hadn't."

Carl shrugged. He didn't say anything. He felt like mentioning the year he lived in Detroit.

"I feel fine," she said, before he could think of how to begin. "Actually, I feel about a hundred percent."

"Bad crop of grapes," he said.

She seemed to be fiddling with the belt of her robe. Carl looked down to his bare feet. When he looked in her direction again, Christine had opened the robe. She wore white panties dotted with dollar signs, a cream-colored brassiere. She said, "Come on, man, I'm depressed. I want to feel better. I used mouthwash in the bathroom." She bent her knees, reached down to push off her panties. She tossed them to one side of the bed. Then, she put her knees apart so he could see all of her.

He supposed it was a test of sorts, because she could not possibly want to. Carl's eyes went from her patch of pubic hair to her eyes. She was not pleading with him, not at all. He wanted to, but not as much as he might have. "Take off your shirt," she said. "I want to see your arms."

"All right," Carl said. He pulled off the shirt he was wearing, and then combed his hair over with his hand.

"Take your time," she said.

Carl gestured. "What is that plastic thing on the wall?"

Christine lifted her head. "What?"

Carl pointed to the wall behind her. Christine lifted herself using her elbows. She turned her head and then looked back to him. "Radio."

"It has the shape of a fried egg with a little nose sticking out of it." He touched at the tip of his own nose.

She reached up and lifted the smooth, odd-shaped thing from the wall. It was an inch thick, had curved sides, a coated wire tail. She moved her finger along an edge of the radio. Then music played, classical. "It's a Moosk radio, Carl. It's sort of shaped like a face, see? The speaker there, that can be the mouth." She wiggled the tail. "Antenna. Cool, huh? Open your mouth and music comes out?"

"Definitely," he said.

With the music on, she reached up, hung the radio on its peg. "I like modern things when I can afford them. You know those two clear plastic chairs out there? They're called Ghost Chairs. Phillipe Starck. Same guy who designed them designed this radio. Well, the chairs are knock-offs actually."

"Knock-off Ghost Chairs?" he said. "I can't live like this, Christine."

She watched him for a time. She said, "Music okay?"

"Yeah," he said. "Who is that?"

"Mendelssohn. Maybe."

He shrugged. "Sounds right."

"Come on over here, Carl," she said. "Let's not make love. But I want you to take off your clothes. Lie down next to me in the bed."

Carl felt relieved. This sounded better than anything. For a time, they both lay on their backs. Christine tied her robe closed again and she breathed in an even way. In fact, after a time, she lay so still on her side of the bed, Carl thought she had gone to sleep. Then she said, "Okay, tell me how it works."

Carl cut his eyes in the direction of their feet. His went beyond her knees but not all the way to her ankles. His size presented him with significant advantages. He always wanted to appreciate this. "You know the racetrack, Christine," he said. "There are no sure things. I think that we should always keep this in mind. Another thing you need to know is that I do not gamble, myself. Back in the day, I did. But it absolutely kills my concentration when I am riding. I get a little panicky when I have a bet down. So I will not be betting with you. You won't be running bets for me or anything like that." He paused for a time. She did not speak and he wanted to say things in an exact way. "I am just going to ride and win races. That's all I am going to think about. I am going to come back to this apartment every night, eat a can of tuna fish, watch the Stanley Cup playoffs or whatever is on, and then I am going to sleep in this bed." He held up a finger. "But, I digress."

He felt Christine smile at this, or it felt like a smile to him. He did not turn to check.

He lowered his hand, let it fall to his chest. "This is what I think should happen," he said. "I finish working horses in the mornings around ten thirty. I will drive back to the apartment and have coffee with you. We will have coffee at the little table in the other room there, where you got sick this morning. Then I will tell you about the horses I am riding that afternoon. I'm not going to say things like 'Bet it all' to you, Christine, because that's ignorant—that's not a smart way to go. That will put all kinds of pressure on everything. I will tell you everything I know. But I do not want to know much about your betting. You know how to read the *Racing Form*. You told me that your husband was a gambler and that he told you that he knew everything about it. But with me, you need to figure things out for yourself. I'll tell you what I know about the horses I am scheduled to ride. You look over the races. You'll have an advantage over practically everyone betting the races. You are living with a jockey, a jockey who is riding some live horses. An advantage is what I can offer you. You've lived with a gambler, you know what a mistake it is to get worked up, get impatient, try to make a fortune. Some days not to play at all might be the smartest thing."

"You are talking like it's already been decided that you will be staying here," she said.

"Hasn't it been?"

When she did speak, she said, "So riders don't gamble? Not all that much?"

"If you are riding in races every day, you can't worry about that," Carl said. "If you are riding regular, you are making money. I thought I would advance you my share of two months' rent. That's the money you can start to play with. What kind of rent do you pay here?"

"Four fifty," she said.

"Okay, I'll advance you three months' rent. That's what, six seventy-five? The meet opens next Saturday. We'll have our coffee together, and I'll tell you what I know. After that, I'll take a shower, get dressed and drive back to the track. The rest of it is up to you." He clenched his toes on both feet, then relaxed them again. "I thought you would like this, actually."

"I suppose I might," Christine's voice said. "Tell me what a jockeys' locker room looks like. I've wondered about that."

He said, "There is a lot of equipment a jockey has to wear. Boots, jockstrap, Kevlar vest, helmet, goggles, silks, riding pants..." His voice trailed off and he didn't say anything for a time.

"It sounds like a Mad Max character."

"Horse falls on you it really doesn't matter, though. I think a lot of it is a state of mind. Just telling yourself you are ready for anything."

"Welcome to Bartertown," she said.

Carl laughed a little with her. "Lockers are full of equipment, boots are lined up on top of the lockers. The valets help you keep track of everything. During a race day, it's an anthill. We are well-trained monkeys. Everyone in there knows what to do."

"How do you guys huddle together to fix races?"

"Christine," he said. He knew she would listen. "I remember a story back from when I was just a kid. There was a *Sports Illustrated* cover story on a guy over in Pennsylvania who fixed a lot of races at Penn National and in New York. The guy had connections in jocks' quarters everywhere. It was organized. The FBI was on to him before the story broke and they had wire taps in the jockeys' rooms in New York. In the story, a few jockeys were singled out. But the story was that the FBI had everybody dead to rights. Every jockey there. They didn't let all that out because it would have killed the sport. That's always what I heard. I don't doubt it." He looked over at her. "I haven't been a part of anything like that for a while because I haven't been riding in a lot of races. Not until last fall. The way they do it now is they just send you a text message from a disposable cell phone. The text doesn't say much. Something like, 'Hold your ride in the seventh today.' The agents set up some of the races. I had a call from an agent the other day and the only reason I didn't suspect him of something like this was that the meet hasn't started as yet."

"What did the agent want?"

"To represent me."

There was a pause and she said, "That's good, right?"

"Yeah, I guess so. But I'm gonna just handle things myself. If I turn into Johnny Velazquez or something, maybe I'll get an agent. Maybe I'll get two. For the time being, I want you."

She finally said, "It sounds to me like what you really want is for me to sit at the table and just listen to you talk."

He said, "I like you, Christine. I really do."

"You can show me how much in a little while."

Carl waved his hand in the air. "No problem."

He heard her laugh.

He said, "You'll beg me for it."

"No, I won't."

In a while, he said, "You feel better now?"

"I guess I do. Look, man, I gotta go to work. I think I am going to take a nap first."

"I think I will, too," he said. "I'm beat."

"I'll set the alarm for three," she said.

Carl felt like he could sleep longer, but he did not say that. He closed his eyes. He was going to spend the spring here, he felt positive about that. He did not want to say anything else.

5.

A few days later, Carl had moved the remainder of his personal belongings into Christine's apartment. He had clothes, a box of boots, a box of other riding gear—chaps, spurs, and four helmets. He was a small man who never needed much to keep him going. Carl's mother had never married and when she gave birth he was three months early, weighed four and a half pounds. His mother left him with her parents and moved out west, to Nevada, he was told later. She told her parents she would send for baby Carl when she got settled. This was what they told him. Carl was six years old, the smallest boy in his class, when the family received news that his mother had died in Reno. She checked into an expensive hotel there, the Paramount, ordered room service for three straight days, then was found hanging in the shower. The police suspected foul play. When his mother's father received the news, he sat in an armchair and held onto the arms of it. He seemed to stay in this exact position for a long time. She killed herself, Loretta, he said to his wife. That she was at a good hotel tells me all I need to know.

The funeral service took place at the public cemetery in Burgundy. A bright fall afternoon where the leaves on the trees were the colors of pumpkins and peaches. After this, when Carl lay in bed at night, his grandmother stood in the doorway of his room. She held her hands together and said the Lord's Prayer. She didn't ask him to say it with her and this eventually bothered him more than anything. When Carl turned sixteen and he told his grandparents of his racetrack plans, his grandfather's eyes appeared to moisten, but then they turned dry again. His grandparents each passed away when Carl was in his twenties and riding in Southern Illinois. He attended his grandfather's funeral but missed his grandmother's because he had three rides that afternoon at Balmoral Park.

The boxes he unpacked at Christine's held something he'd won in a poker game: a set of blinkers supposedly once worn by Run Dusty Run. The hood and the plastic half-cups around the eye holes were bright yellow. The card game had taken place in a tack room, and another rider, Martin Arnold, wanted to use the set of blinkers as currency. Carl okayed the play. He thought Run Dusty Run had raced in the mid-seventies, had chased Seattle Slew throughout the Triple Crown one year. Carl won the hand, won the blinkers. When Carl looked up photos of Run Dusty Run on the Internet, the horse never wore blinkers. Arnold was always in trouble and he left town a couple of days after the game. Carl supposed that when he saw Arnold again that they'd straighten things out. Maybe a year after the card game, Arnold was riding at Fort Erie in Canada and one night he just disappeared. Body never found. There were stories, rumors that he was into a loan shark or about to spill on how the mob was fixing races up there. Arnold wasn't a bad guy, and he had probably misjudged the wrong person.

Carl liked the blinkers. They gave him the feeling that even when things were going badly in his life, on the whole he'd still gotten off pretty easy.

Carl brought a milk crate of records, CDs, and DVDs, and a two-month-old flat-screen TV he thought might replace the set Christine had. There was a disagreement about the set. Christine said it was way too large and she didn't watch that much television anyway. Carl's TV was expensive and he didn't want to just throw it out. The next morning, Carl put the flat-screen in the back of his wheezy Ford Focus and drove it over to Summit Park. He carried the TV into the jocks' room, told a valet named Drew McCauley he needed to sell it and that he would split the proceeds. Drew was in his fifties and shaped like a bowling ball. He looked at the set as if Carl had placed an original Matisse in front of him. Drew said, "We can get something good for this." Carl clapped him on the shoulder.

Carl had been on the road since age sixteen and he had learned something about moving: if you owned too many things, you would never understand when it was time to go. By Thursday, two days before the start of the Summit meet, Carl had completely moved in with Christine. He made out a check for $675—his half of three months' rent—and left it for her next to his printer on the kitchen table. He walked into the bedroom and was surprised to see Bo stretched out on the middle of the bed. The cat's tail smacked at the bedspread. Carl wondered if Bo was now ready to be friends. He sat on the edge of the bed and reached over to scratch Bo's head. Bo allowed Carl to do this. The cat's eyes seemed like a vortex, a passage to something else. Then Bo sat upright and Carl drew back his hand. "Ow," the cat said. Carl reached over to pet the cat's head again. Bo poked at Carl's hand with his right front paw but kept his claws withdrawn. Carl felt glad, and he thought about texting Christine.

Carl finally stopped petting Bo's head. He sat with his hands on his knees. "Thank you," he said.

On the opening day of the meeting, it began to rain before sunrise. While Christine slept, Carl pulled on his slickers in the bathroom. He drove to a florist after morning workouts and bought a bunch of daisies. When he opened the door to the apartment, she was seated at the kitchen table. Christine stayed quiet as he walked over and held the flowers out to her. She said, "Look how dry you are. How many umbrellas do you own?"

"Coffee?" he said. "I have slickers. Two sets."

"I'll make you a cup."

"Here, take these."

She reached her hands forward. From the cupboard, Christine brought out a vase of sky-blue glass that looked like a large test tube and a slight-looking wooden rack to set it in. The vase was on the table, the flowers were in the vase. Carl began to talk about the horses he was scheduled to ride today. Christine produced a small notepad, perhaps from the pocket of her robe, and held it on her lap. Carl talked and she wrote. When he paused, she looked up. She held the pen away from the pad and her expression was like, This okay? Carl said, "In the fourth race today, I'm on a horse named White Star Line..." His eyes went to the windows. Mist had formed around the edges of the frames and beyond the glass the falling rain had a silvery quality. "What are you wearing today?" he said.

"What?" she said. She touched at the belt of her robe. "Underwear? Look, Carl..."

"What are you wearing to the track today?"

Christine folded both of her hands over the notebook. She had a look of patience about her. "What's the problem?"

"Nothing," he said.

"You don't like to ride in the slop?" she said. One of her hands moved across the opened page of the notebook. "I don't blame you at all."

"I've ridden in the mud from here to Edmonton," he said.

"What then?"

"Nothing," he said.

"Okay."

"It's just that when I pictured some of this, I saw it a certain way. I saw you in a sundress and a spring hat walking for a betting window. You wore sunglasses, high heels. You stepped up to the window, named the bets you wanted to make and then when the teller told you how much, you took out hundred-dollar bills and handed them over. You weren't carrying any goddamn notebook." Carl decided not to say anything else. Since the first moment he had approached her with the idea of living together, Carl had not taken a tone with Christine. She had been mysterious and testy at times, but this was predictable because she was young and getting used to their situation. Those moments meant nothing to him. On race days, however, things needed to be different. When it was time to ride in races, Carl wanted to have a certain attitude about everything. He needed to think a certain way and he even wanted to sound a certain way.

Christine said, "Carl, this is Cleveland."

"Living in Cleveland means you have to write everything down?"

She watched him for a time. Then she said, "Sundress?"

"It doesn't matter."

Christine pointed the tip of her pen to the notebook page. "Fourth race, White Star Line. Go."

Carl said, "He's a real tall horse." He watched the rain falling. "I rode him a couple of times last November. He tries hard in his races, but he's just a grinder. Has absolutely no speed at all. When the track is real fast, the others get away from him in a hurry. I worked him the other morning and he felt pretty solid. Right now, they're keeping the track deep because it's early in the meet. Helps the horses get fit faster. Doesn't beat 'em up like a fast track might. With this rain, it'll be a swamp... he ought to handle it better than the others."

By the fourth race that afternoon, the rain had stopped. The sky above looked like burned-up charcoal. Since leaving the apartment, Carl had tried not to think about Christine. He sat atop White Star Line and the horse stood quietly in the starting gate. Carl had six sets of goggles strapped across his eyes, one atop the other. White Star Line was never in a hurry early in a race; they'd be covered in mud ten seconds in. He'd peel away one set, then a furlong later, have to peel away another. To start, these goggles would fog his view but that was all right. He and this horse knew their way around.

Once the gates opened, the horses broke in a line and those inside of White Star Line went for the lead. Grainy layers of mud slapped against Carl's face. His top set of goggles was almost instantly useless, but he didn't pull them down. Carl tasted mud, swallowed it. White Star line aimed for the outer rail in an attempt to escape the mud shower, and Carl let the horse drift to the outside of the others, then yanked down his top set of goggles. White Star Line could feel some escape there and it eased the horse's jerky stride. Carl tapped its neck with the whip and they began to race straight up the backstretch. With a half mile to run, White Star Line had almost lost touch with the field, but as the runners made for the far turn, one horse, then another, began to drift back. White Star Line's stride felt like little more than a breast-stroke, but when they inched past a third horse Carl's insides lightened. He kept his mount in the middle of the track for the run down the homestretch and he stayed busy. White Star Line had been running on the left lead, with the left hoof hitting the ground just beyond the right, but Carl tossed the reins at the horse, gave the subtlest tug on the right rein and White Star Line switched to the right lead, found a burst of energy there. Carl worked methodically, and he knew he was going to win the race. He tried not think about Christine. Yet, he thought about the shape of her face. He hollered at his horse, "Yahhhh!" They made the lead fifty yards from the wire and held on to win by a half-length. Carl galloped out White Star Line, then eased him into a jog. His horse was ready for these commands. Finally, White Star Line returned to a walk.

An icy wind sailed down the backstretch. He turned his horse and they cantered back around the clubhouse turn. The glassed-in grandstand seemed to be glowing like a pumpkin now. He could not picture Christine at all then—all he envisioned were mostly empty rows, the few gamblers there having already turned to the next race. She could check the results on her break, on the boss's computer. The results would pop up and there would be *White Star Line, Arvo, C.* and that feeling would hit her. It was just another cheap, forgettable race at a racetrack one rung from the end of the world, but she had this one. By God she had this one. Carl moved his tongue over his teeth, spat out a spoonful of mud. A mud-painted jockey named Alice Saylor trotted her little gray mount back to be unsaddled and Carl said in her direction, "Lucky to win anything today!"

"This is somebody's nightmare!" Saylor said, sounding a lot farther away than she was.

Carl bobbed in the saddle, in rhythm to his horse's stride. There was an opening in the outside railing and he guided White Star Line in that direction. Two guards stood out on the track holding the portable section, their slickers dripping with greasy-looking mud. In the direction of the stewards' booth at the top of the grandstand, Carl gave a flick of the whip, a silent signal he'd had a clear trip. Adjacent to the saddling ring, the winner's circle was a half moon of scrubby Astroturf, ringed by shrubbery that was three feet high and still, brown-black with winter. Carl smiled in the direction of the photographer as he sat on White Star Line, and the camera's flash brought a sudden saffron glow to things. Just as quickly it was gone again.

That night in the apartment, Carl slept on and off. He thought of the sounds of hoofbeats as they raced through the mud; how close to perfect his life could be. He awakened when Christine arrived home from work. She closed the front door and it sounded as if she were walking in a quiet-as-possible way across the living room. Then there came the pop of a wine cork. He couldn't keep himself from getting out of the bed and he walked out to the edge of the living room. Christine sat in one of the plastic chairs at the kitchen table and the overheard light was on there. Carl could not tell if she had heard his footsteps. He said, "Bo came out to see me a couple of days ago. He laid on the bed and let me pet him." She had heard, he supposed, because it took her a moment to turn her head.

"I had a talk with him," she said.

"Did you get it good?"

"Yeah," she said. "I sure did. Want to hear about it? How much I bet, what I wore when I did it?"

"You wore a sundress," he said. He tapped at the side of his head. "And I'm going back to bed."

"Come over here," she said. He eyed the loveseat, decided to move in that direction. She stood, walked over. She held her wine glass and stood in front of him. "What do you think ought to happen now?"

"Do I seem sexier?"

Christine leaned forward, held out her glass and he accepted it. He took a sip and she pulled her long-sleeve polo over her head. She wore a shiny, royal-blue brassiere. She decided to sit down on the edge of a cushion by him. She put out her hand and he passed the glass to her. She said, "I'm not good at this."

"Yes, you are," he said. "You're wonderful."

She watched him, then she said, "I'm ready."

A few hours later, Carl was up again. He walked out to the living room and listened for the sound of rain outside, but there was nothing like that going on. As he had the day before and the day before that, Carl had laid out his work clothes on the loveseat. They were folded in a short stack there. He carried them into the bathroom and dressed quietly. He pulled on his down vest and left the apartment.

6.

Carl and Christine had coffee together every morning when he arrived home from the racetrack. On Mondays, Christine didn't have to work. Tuesdays and Wednesdays there was no racing at Summit Park, so Carl had these afternoons to himself. Her gambling went positively on the horses he rode. Carl was off to an excellent start. In the first two weeks, he guided home nine winners, good enough for third in the jockey standings. He didn't ask how much she made or lost from day to day. He didn't need to know. But he could tell she was pleased about how things were going. She didn't seem to mind being in bed with him at all.

In the last week of March, on a Tuesday morning, she not only mentioned her husband, she began to talk about him. She and Carl sat at the kitchen table in the clear plastic chairs. There was no racing this day and Carl felt quiet and open to just about anything. They talked for a time about gambling and patience. She began to talk about her former husband's gambling, and his losing.

Christine's former husband was Michael Fleming. Michael had grown up on the west side of Cincinnati. The men in his family were gamblers. His father and uncle owned a taproom with a basement casino that featured poker tables and a roulette wheel. They operated a profitable bookmaking operation. As a kid, Michael had worked weekends, brought drinks to the players, and his father allowed him to bet part of his tip money on one roulette spin every night. It was by far the most important part of his childhood, this one roulette spin. Once he won $175 and when he did, somebody brought him a cold bottle of beer.

Michael didn't want to do anything else with his life but gamble. He understood that he would have to work and earn money, but the kind of work he did was of minimal importance. When he began dating Christine, he talked about his gambling in a matter-of-fact way. He said the one benefit of being exposed to gambling at such a young age was that he had seen right away all the trouble compulsive and out-of-control gambling could bring to someone's life. It would not affect him, not even if he played every day.

Christine met Michael at a small college in Indiana that they both attended. He was already a bit notorious on campus when she arrived there as a freshman. On one occasion, he had returned from a weekend trip to Cincinnati with two black eyes and a broken nose. The gossip was that a collector for a bookmaker had done this. When they started dating, Michael tried to impress her with the fact that he always knew the point spread of any game. He would say, Go ahead and ask me about Houston versus Atlanta. He was sort of crazy, and he loved Bill Murray movies. She couldn't tell when he had a bet going because he watched all sports events on television in a stony way.

She learned that it was all right to ask him if he had money on a particular game. If a player fumbled, he might say, There goes your wedding band, sweetheart. Christine didn't develop a sense of humor about Michael's gambling; she did not believe this was necessary. He would tell her, Where I grew up, there were no women like you, Christine. He said things like this to her often. She believed there was an entirely different person in him that wanted to come out.

He graduated ahead of her, took a job out in Indianapolis as a rep for industrial detergents. She quit school, moved in with him. Michael and Christine lived in Indianapolis together for three years. When he received a promotion to route manager, he proposed to her. Before they were married, she decided to have a talk with Michael about his gambling. They sat up in bed together one night in their small apartment in downtown Indianapolis and she explained to Michael that she loved him deeply and that in one way it would never matter what he would do or what he would say. Part of her heart was already given over to him forever. But, it was absolutely critical that he never hide anything from her. She did not need to know about every little piece of business he was up to. But, if he was on a losing streak, he needed to talk to her. Christine said, I can always make you feel better, you have to trust in this. Gambling is the unknown thing in our lives. It is the one thing I am unsure about. Because of this, you always need to be completely honest about it.

Her father was particularly concerned about Michael's problem. On several occasions, her father said that until he had a serious talk with Michael, he could never allow Christine to marry him. Christine begged her father not to do this. She said she'd already had a serious talk with Michael and that was enough. Her father insisted, however, and Christine eventually stopped arguing with him about it, partly because she wasn't certain her serious talk with Michael had made the impression she'd wanted it to. She had put her heart and soul into that talk. Perhaps Michael needed something else.

All right, Daddy, she said at last. If it's what you have to do.

I have to, her father said.

Once she agreed to let him talk to Michael, her father didn't bring up the subject again. Whenever she brought Michael to her hometown on a Sunday afternoon, they had dinner with her parents at one of the restaurants off the interstate ramp. Everyone was polite. Of course, this was depressing. Christine's mother, who'd been present every time her father had insisted he needed to have a talk with Michael, never said much of anything. It was expected at these gatherings that Christine would do much of the talking. She was what they all had in common. She even would edge towards the subject of gambling.

They held the wedding in Christine's hometown, the event cheered by her family and her friends. Everyone knew how much she loved him. Michael grinned and shook hands; Christine was hugged by everyone, some of them acting like they didn't want to let go. Confidence filled the air; she would handle his flaws. At the time, she felt like the strongest person in town, in the entire state of Indiana.

They tried to have children but could not and they agreed not to find out which of them had the fertility issue. If they really wanted children, they could adopt. But they decided not to do this, either. Michael made good money at his job. Christine didn't have to work, but she part-timed as a substitute high school teacher. She exercised daily. She liked to paint still-lifes, though she didn't often show these works to Michael because he could never figure out how to compliment her without sounding patronizing.

Michael lost his job in the spring of 2008; he had seen the warning signs in his business, yet he reassured Christine a possible recession would not affect them. Their marriage had been steady to this point. They had a savings account and he had an IRA. Michael had pledged to be honest when it came to his gambling. They both had access to all of their accounts. He had been a stout George W. Bush man, though Michael did not defend the president's policies after he lost his job. Michael's outlook changed dramatically. He said, Maybe the Iraqis were right, we are the devil. Look around: if you are not greedy, you cannot prosper in this country. The twenty-first century is the beginning of the end. She thought he would spiral like this for just a while. Then he would regain his balance. He was a gambler. He was well-acquainted with reversals of fortune.

Wasn't he?

Michael became a relentless cheapskate. He began to grill Christine about ordinary household expenses. She applied for a full-time teaching job at one of the public schools and received a one-year contract. Michael began to do the grocery shopping. In the evenings, he showed her the receipts, pointed out the money he had saved. Christine saw where things were heading and she thought they both needed to apply for graduate school. They needed to start over, and they needed to do this right away. They were in their twenties—only their mid-twenties—and everything was still in front of them. She pressed him on the issue of graduate school but he would not commit to it. School will always be there. That was all he really had to say about the matter.

One afternoon she arrived home from her teaching job and when she opened the door, Michael stood in the middle of their living room. He held a champagne bottle and when he saw her, he popped the cork. Christine felt like she had been punched in the throat. She knew Michael. The foam ran down the side of the bottle and onto Michael's hand. He held the bottle in the air. I have it all figured out, he said. I am flying out to Las Vegas, Christine. I'm going to bet eighteen thousand on one game. Texas Tech versus Oklahoma. I have been wanting to do this for a long time. We win, I won't have to work for a whole year.

While he was still holding the bottle, Christine said, What will you do then, sweetheart?

He tried to hold his smile. He said, Professional gambler. It's my dream, he said. You know that.

Yes, Christine said. I do.

Michael finally lowered the bottle. In his other hand he held two champagne flutes. He said, I want you to go to Las Vegas with me. Show your support.

No, she said.

This will be the most important bet I will make in my life, he said.

Christine was exhausted. It was spring and her students were restless. She said, You'll say that again, Michael. Over and over. She tried to smile. She wanted to be kind.

Michael held the champagne bottle and the glasses and he didn't say anything else. But his eyes said terrible things to her.

Christine and Carl sat at the kitchen table with the late-morning sun streaming in. She said, "Michael is supposed to be a gambler. He's never wanted to understand anything more than this. There's just this whole other side to gambling, though. A whole other world." Carl didn't know what to say and he didn't add anything. She looked at him squarely and said, "It has nothing to do with the size of your balls."

"What's wrong with the size of my balls?"

"I just said nothing."

"I would hope not."

"It takes guts to ride in races," she said. "Betting is something else, though. You have to listen."

Carl lifted his coffee mug. "Look at you."

"Once I finally kicked him out, I got interested in gambling. I was always afraid of it when he was living here. Maybe he was just doing it wrong. There has to be a way, you know?"

Carl nodded. He had been married twice and in some ways Christine could not compete with either of his two wives. The promises he and Christine had made to one another were modest. Carl could be a good man, but Christine would never want to marry him—he was positive of that. He did not want to even think about marrying her. This was why he couldn't compete with Michael, even though Michael was a compulsive gambler, a bum, a waste of space.

Carl said, "Let me make love to you right now, Christine. Then let's go back to sleep for a while."

"I just woke up," she said.

"I'll make love to you and I'll go back to sleep."

"If you want to go to the bedroom and wait for me, that's all right, Carl. I might be in there in a while."

Carl stood and carried his coffee mug over to the kitchen sink. He walked across the living room floor, into the short hallway that led to the bedroom. He ducked into the bathroom. He took off his clothes, stood under the lukewarm water of the shower, then dried himself, combed his hair, folded his clothes under one arm, lifted his boots, wiggled one hand forward, opened the door and stepped into the hallway. When he opened the door to the bedroom, he hoped that Christine would be in bed, waiting for him. But it turned out that he was in the bedroom by himself. He wouldn't have minded if Bo appeared. The cat could lie at his side and Carl could scratch its head. "Bo," Carl said. But he didn't expect anything.

By the time Christine came in, Carl was tucked under the covers, almost asleep. She climbed under the covers and began to stroke him and they were murmuring to one another when he thought he heard her say, "Oh, Michael." Carl's eyes were closed at that moment and he only opened them again when he felt her getting on top of him. She placed her hands on his shoulders and gave him a shove. "Call me whatever you want to," Christine said. She started to move atop him. "While we are doing this."

"No," he said.

She closed her eyes and said, "Come on."

"Christine." She pushed down on his shoulders. His hands reached for her thighs. It was like when he was riding in a race—Carl didn't want to think about anything. He said, "Alycia."

"There you go," she said. "Ah."

"Alycia," he said. He did not say it again, though. He reached for Christine's arms, and held on to them just below the elbows.

Afterward, she eased herself from him and lay flat on her back on the bed. Christine laughed, then she seemed to just want to even out her breathing. "Alycia?" she said.

He had one hand behind his head, his legs too sore for him to hold them straight. He turned to one side, bent both knees and felt more comfortable. "My second wife," he said. "I wasn't really thinking about her, though."

"I wasn't really thinking about Michael," she said. "I just said his name. I've said it so often. Michael. He prefers it to 'Mike.' He says Mike is a salesman's name."

Carl decided to think about the race he had won on that muddy track on opening day atop White Star Line. Once the field had turned into the homestretch, Carl had steered the horse into the center of the track so they could have a clear path to the finish. He knew they were going to win the race and his mind went to something other than riding his horse. He pictured Christine. They were just starting out, he had just moved in with her.

He said, "I think things are going well. I think it's all right to say someone else's name. Not too much, though."

"Agreed."

He said, "Alycia was a nice lady. Religious lady. I almost gave up riding for her. My first wife, Kelly, raised my kids. They live over in Akron. They thought the racetrack made me crazy. I am glad they stayed away from it. There are all kinds of lives out there."

"How did you two meet?"

"I met Alycia in a supermarket," he said, and then he laughed a bit. "I don't remember what I was in there for."

"Wine and tuna fish, obviously."

"Probably," he said.

It was quiet then and right before she spoke again, Carl could feel her draw in a breath. "We have a problem," she said.

"It's too early for that."

"Oh, foo," she said. "Michael knows. He knows about you living here."

"So?"

"Someone at the Seven Seas told him. I think he followed me to the racetrack one day last week. Stayed away, at a distance. But I could feel him there. He denied it, of course."

"You..."

"He stopped by the bar last night. He tried not to be a jerk. But I guess he was. He wants in. He wants a piece of the action."

Wrong, Carl thought. "He screwed up things really bad, didn't he? Did he hit you? Did he abuse you?"

In a moment, she said, "No. He lost his all-or-nothing bet in Las Vegas, of course. When he got home, he got a tape of the game and watched it over and over. I got him to throw it away and then we decided we would just move, leave Indiana for good. He wanted to go north, I wanted to go south. We wound up in Detroit. He worked for a vending-machine company there. He studied the races night and day. He hung around with racetrack people. He paid them money for inside info, tips on live horses. But nothing ever worked out. We left Detroit owing three months' rent. We moved here. Things came apart fast. I'm not going to tell you anything more, though. One time he did grab at my hair. The next day, he moved out. I really don't know what he's doing for money right now. I don't want to know. I just see him at the bar. Racetrackers hang out at the Seven Seas. I guess that's the draw."

Carl did not say anything.

A minute later, Christine said, "I used to think gambling was just dangerous and pretty crazy." Her voice thinned out.

Carl decided to lie flat on his back now. He rested his hands on his breastbone. "When you gamble, you absolutely must try to keep your emotions out of it. You can't have a chip on your shoulder."

"Michael is aware of this, I would hope," she said. "Maybe he isn't. He doesn't question enough. He's lived in the Midwest his whole life." Christine rolled to one side, faced him. She put her hand along her jawbone, rested her elbow on the pillow. She was nude, and the color of her skin made him think of sand dunes. Right at this moment he wished that he were married to Christine, but he hoped he didn't look that way to her. He wished that his winning would go on forever. He felt the urge to blurt out something like a confession. Instead, he let his eyes travel down the length of her body and then back again. This was what she wanted, and it was all right with him.

Carl said, "You're saying that he is going to cause trouble."

"We have to deal with him, Carl. He is not going to go away. I warned you about this."

"You did. You want him to go away, Christine? I don't think I've heard you say as much."

She cut her eyes, glanced in the direction of her feet. Then she looked directly at Carl. "He and I are walking through the ruins," she said. "We're probably done. But I am not over every little thing, you know? I just want you to know that Michael is around. I wonder if we shouldn't let him in on something."

"Why?"

Her eyes flared, then dimmed. "I'd like to see the fucking guy win something for once." She brushed at something on the bedcovers that Carl did not see. "Is that so hard to believe? I just don't want to lie to you about anything." She shrugged. "You've been nice to me."

Carl clenched his right hand into half a fist and looked at his fingernails. He let his arm fall to the covers. He wondered if he oughtn't set Christine straight on a couple of things. Home life for Carl needed to be peaceful and steady in order for him to ride well. The melodrama of relationships and families obliterated his focus. This would result in nothing but losers at the track. Maybe her ex would stop following her around if that happened. It was an intriguing angle, though he understood it was not an honest assessment of things. Carl was going to win races this year, he was going to wind up as one of the top riders of the meet. He wanted to live with Christine while this happened. That was all he wanted. Carl said, "I'm not interested in worrying about this guy, Christine. You think you can handle him?"

"Well," she said. "No. I'm afraid I haven't been clear with you. See, I'm concerned about him. But I am more concerned about me." She touched the blue bed covers with the tip of her index finger. "I am making money. I am making some money. I like what you and I have. And I don't want to see it get messed up."

"You want me to talk to him?"

"You're the rider," she said. "You've got control of this thing."

Carl liked how this sounded. He thought, Very good, Christine. "I don't have control over much. Maybe you're the one who hasn't been listening."

"Carl," she said. She didn't say anything else until he turned to see her. "Be kind to him, okay? He's a gambler."

"I agreed to this?"

In a second, she said, "I didn't hear you say yes. But, you are here. I am here. And, so is Michael."

"I guess so," he said.

"You needed to know," she said. "Maybe you can help."

7.

Despite the talk of Michael, Carl had an excellent week of riding. On Thursday, another rainy day where the track turned to gravy, Carl had three runner-up finishes—two on long shots. The trifecta payoffs in these races were in the thousands for just a two-dollar bet. The next morning, following workouts, Christine rubbed his shoulders and later she walked in on him taking a shower. She turned off the water, stepped in, and put both of her hands on the towel rack. He almost lost his footing at one point. He grabbed for the soap dish. It took a while for them to finish and after they did they dried off and went to bed. They fell asleep on top of the covers. When Carl awakened again, Christine was sleeping on her back and he watched her. Without opening her eyes, she said, "Carl?"

"Yes?"

"I ran into Mrs. Lovain at the Food Lion yesterday. Do you know who I am referring to?"

"No."

"The woman who lives in one of the apartments across the alley. She said you are watching her. She tried to say it more tactfully than that. She said, 'Chris, I didn't know you had a new fella living with you.' I said, 'Oh, yes.' She gave me one of those polite smiles after that. I had to think for a second about what she was really trying to tell me."

"Tell her to close her blinds if she doesn't want people to see her."

"The apartments on this side of that building are pretty small. I'm sure she feels boxed in."

"She lives alone. I don't watch her undress or anything. Good lord."

"She's over fifty."

"I've been on the racetrack my whole life. What am I missing? I wonder about that. I wonder what a different kind of life has to offer."

"There's nothing in it at all," she said. Her face turned in his direction. "Zero."

"You gonna stay away from that?"

"It got to me and Michael," she said. "We weren't ready. In a way, I hope we never will be."

Carl said quickly, "Me neither. Look, what's Mrs. What'sherface do? I was thinking she is a librarian or something."

"She's adjunct at Cleveland State. She gets an alimony from her ex. When it was hot last summer and there weren't any guys in either of our apartments, we'd open windows and talk. It was neat. I felt quite citified," she said. "Where do you watch her from?"

"Our table. I sit there in the evenings and work on my computer. I look over and there she is. She arrives home, goes straight for the wine, then disappears, returns in a sweatshirt and jeans. She has really nice gray hair. She makes herself something in the microwave, eats at her table. Reads the paper. Has another glass of wine. She takes her time doing everything. It's all right. It's not too bad."

"If there was a man over there, would you watch?"

"Men generally aren't as interesting. Are they?"

"Actually, they are." She laid her arms at her sides.

Something inside Carl tensed. He was not going to be enough for this woman. He said, "Do you want me to stop looking over at her?"

"No." She reached over, touched the covers by his hip. "Of course not. But I want you to know that she sees you."

Carl won the last two races on the card that afternoon. The next day he took the feature, an overnight handicap aboard a nervous little mare named Royal Harmony. The subject of Michael didn't come up again until the following Tuesday morning. Christine mentioned joining an athletic club but wondered how she could find the time to work out regularly, and then, after the slightest pause, she said, "He followed me to the track on Sunday. I picked up his khaki-colored Toyota in traffic about a mile away from Summit. He didn't even bother to hide. He drove behind me into the parking lot. He waited for me to get out of my car and start walking for the track before he got out of his. Inside, I tried to find a different pari-mutuel clerk, but it's always the same old goddamn faces in there. He's friends with some of the clerks, I guess. I started to get confused, so I just walked to a window, made my bets, and got out of there. I didn't even collect my winnings from the day before."

"How'd you do on Sunday?"

"I didn't bet that favorite you won on," she said. "I didn't think he'd carry his speed like that. Even you had your doubts."

"I did," Carl said, then leaned back in his chair. "But I am one mean-riding monkey right now, Christine. You need to accept that. You're putting some of your winnings away, I hope."

"Of course. I also cleared out the bottom drawer in the bureau in case you need that. I started a bank account for you."

"You did what?"

"You don't want more space?"

"I need another drawer. I mean the bank account. I already have a bank account."

"Now you have another. Surprise."

"Did he say anything to you?"

"As I walked away from the window, he did. He said, 'I want you.'"

Carl said, "I guess he does."

"He said, 'Help me, Christine.'"

"Jesus Christ." He brought his arms forward, rested them on the table. He circled two fingers around the handle of the mug. "I'll talk to him. While you're at work tomorrow." He thought, What exactly do you want me to say? Carl found himself shaking his head. "Tell him, Jumping Java, the one on Marquette Avenue. Four p.m. If he's one minute late, I'm leaving."

"It might scare him," she said. "He might not want to."

"Well, then we tried, Christine. All right? It's not like we're waterboarding the guy. It's not as if we are madly in love." That last line caused him to stop. Carl made his hand flat and cut into the air with it like a politician. "I will talk to him."

Christine looked at him in a cold way. "I told you once that I am not a whore. Everyone at work thinks that about me now.

Living with a hot jockey. Everyone wants a tip. I try to tell them. I say, 'Look, he doesn't tell me everything.'"

"I tell you what I know for certain."

"People crave sure things. They need to be reassured."

Carl nodded. "You shouldn't worry about what people say."

"I don't," she said. "I am just telling you what I deal with. Goddamnit, when I talk do you listen at all?"

Carl had seen Michael before, at the Seven Seas last fall. A tall, blond man who had walked over to Christine at the bar while Carl had been talking her up. I'll see you later, sweetheart, he'd said. Or, Goodnight, sweetheart. He showed up frequently and Carl hadn't had a good feeling about him even then. At the bar one night, Carl said, Is that guy from Summit Park? A trainer? I don't recognize him.

That's my ex, she said. Then she began to wipe down the counter. Try me again later—okay, Carl? I'm beat.

Carl had insisted Michael be punctual for their meeting at Jumping Java, but Carl himself was fifteen minutes late getting there. He walked in and immediately spotted Michael seated in a leatherette chair by a window with its back to the street. The chair by it had a dish on the seat. Michael had his elbows on the arm rests and was touching the tips of his fingers together. He wore a black blazer and a button-down shirt with the collar open. Carl approached, and as he did, Michael stood and lifted the plate from the seat of the chair next to him. He was tall, taller than Christine. Carl did not put out his hand when he said, "Michael, right?"

"That's right." He placed the plate on the shiny black coffee table at his shins. He straightened, buttoned the second button of his wool blazer. Carl sat in the free chair. Michael unbuttoned his jacket again and sat down. Michael had wavy, long hair that flared out on either side of his neck, scared blue eyes and a prominent nose that looked as if it had been broken on any number of occasions. He had faint freckles under his eyes. He wore faded jeans, sneakers. It wasn't difficult to imagine that women liked him. Carl laid his arms on the arm rests. Music played. Jazz, Chet Baker. "Coffee?" Michael said, motioning in the direction of the counter at the back of the room.

Carl turned partway, twisted his neck. "You having anything?"

"I did," Michael said. "Espresso. Biscotti." He motioned to the plate on the coffee table before them. Carl considered the plate, the crumbs there.

Carl unzipped his jacket then zipped it up halfway. "Yeah, I'm running late today." He glanced around the room, noticed for the first time the size of the crowd. Most of the people seemed to be here by themselves—reading, nipping at their coffees, working on their laptops. Carl said, "Where did you go to school?"

"Indiana," he said. "Small college."

Carl wanted to ask, What are you thinking about right now, Michael? Are you thinking you'd like to beat the hell out of me? Or do you just want to be partners? "With Christine," Carl said, in an absent way.

"A hick school in a hick state," Michael said.

Carl felt the shape of his face change. "I'm trying to make her some money right now."

"That's your main interest, huh?"

Carl did not take his eyes from Michael. "No, it's not." Someone at the next table answered a cell phone and Carl and Michael turned their heads partway. The person on the phone, a teen boy in a denim jacket, had his back to them. Carl said, "Michael."

"What?" Michael said. The kid in denim moved away.

"Yes?" Carl said.

"You said 'Michael.'"

"I did? No, that was a 'Michael' at the end of my sentence. Like 'No, it's not, Michael.'" Carl looked at him. His button-down shirt had a worn collar and he looked disheveled, defeated. Carl had agreed to talk with Michael not because he thought he could really help things but primarily to position himself with Christine as vastly superior to her ex. Now Carl knew this was not possible. Michael was a hapless, unrealistic gambler. When Christine was without him, she was pragmatic, intelligent, kind. But these things were not all a person felt, nor all they desired to.

Michael said, "Where's Big Zip right now?"

"California," Carl said. "They ran him in the Ancient Title Handicap last time. Didn't do any good."

"Seven furlongs is too long for that horse."

"I know that."

"I remember the first time I saw the horse's name in the entries here last year. I thought his name was Big Zit. Maybe they ought to bring him back here, let you ride him again. This is where he belongs."

Carl did not say anything to this. Michael wanted to insult him, perhaps believing Carl was emotionally attached to Big Zip in some way. Carl had ridden thousands of horses; many of them were either mistreated, ignorant, misunderstood, or ill-tempered. Some loved to run and they wanted to run for him. Big Zip had been a rare find on the salvage-yard circuit, and as Carl rode Big Zip to its first victory he knew the horse wouldn't be here for long. He got to ride Big Zip four times in all and was grateful for each opportunity. But he was not emotionally attached to the animal.

Michael puffed his cheeks, then exhaled. He seemed ready to pop up from his chair, but he stayed put. "She thought it would be a good idea if we talked," he said. "She thought maybe we could work out a deal. Turns out she likes making money."

"She's a good player from what I can tell," Carl said. "She listens."

"Are you in love with her?" Michael said in a voice louder than the one he had been using. He kept his eyes straight ahead. "I am." His voice turned quieter. "This is the way it is. You all will never be able to keep me away. I'm already closer than you know."

Sounds like a song, Carl thought. He didn't say this; he didn't need to belittle Michael. It didn't seem necessary. "I'll give you one good tip a month if you will stay away from her."

From the corner of his eye, Carl watched for a change in Michael. The music now was a ballad, a female singer whose voice Carl didn't recognize. "I'll text you," Carl said. "But this isn't going to be any dead lock, Michael. I might listen for info and I'll give you good information. But I don't want to hear it from you if things don't work out. It's a horse race, all right? Don't forget that." Carl folded his hands together, rested them just above his waist. "I sure am not going to give you anything I am riding. Doesn't work out, you'll accuse me of something." After he said that last part, he wished he hadn't.

Michael's voice said, "Stay away?"

Carl tried to concentrate. "Don't go anywhere near the apartment. When Christine is at the windows, stay away. You need to let her concentrate." Carl's voice fell off. He wanted to say something about the bar, too—the Seven Seas. "The second she complains to me about anything, no deal." He listened to the music; the singer had a lovely voice, with an Irish brogue. "You don't have to say yes," Carl said. "Either she'll complain to me or she won't. If I don't hear anything else about it..."

"All right, I get it," Michael said. "But it's like you've been telling me, jock. No promises." He looked in the direction of the window that faced the street. "I don't get it with her and you guys. You jockeys. You're not the first—you know that, right?" Michael's jaw muscles worked. "Did you hear what I just said?"

Carl slowly shook his head, but this was only because he didn't want to talk with Michael anymore. There was nothing left to say.

Michael said, "What is it with you jocks?"

"Don't know."

"You've got an advantage over me. See, you're up on those horses. I don't ride racehorses. My wife is fucking a jockey," he said. Carl wanted to leave then, but something kept him in the chair. Michael shook his head. "We need to get out of this place. Before something really bad happens."

"You need to calm down," Carl said.

"If I was small, I'd be the greatest jockey in the world," Michael said. He didn't turn in Carl's direction for this. "I am fearless. I know how to win."

Carl stood and left the coffee shop. He left Michael there and didn't look back. Carl's heart beat hard in his chest for some reason. He decided to drive to the Seven Seas Tavern and report to Christine about how the meeting had gone. Whatever he would tell her, it would only be the truth. He and Christine had been trying to keep things clear. This had been quite helpful.

Happy Hour wasn't until six, so she'd be able to find a few minutes for him. He would sit at the counter and she could serve him a glass of red wine. Carl hadn't been to the Seven Seas since he'd made up his mind that he wanted to live with Christine. Once he'd decided that, he'd wanted her to see him in a different way than over a bar counter.

Christine had started working there last summer, right before Labor Day—a period when Carl had been struggling to find mounts. He was a journeyman, a rider with nothing special to offer. Carl liked to sit at the bar counter and watch a baseball game with the other horsemen. Some riders, especially successful ones, could make a drink last. Carl liked red wine, how the taste of it could linger. A few sips could hit him pretty hard. He didn't want to be loopy in front of anyone and he didn't want to speak bitterly about anything, which other riders sometimes did. If he had more than a glass he'd have to sweat it out the next morning, put on a sweatsuit and jog a mile around the track after training hours. He was already in good shape.

One Saturday afternoon late last summer, he'd come to the end of another mountless afternoon and decided to drive over to the Seven Seas, find an open seat at the counter, and when he did, Christine, a new hire, stood in front of him. She asked what he wanted. She didn't know that Carl was a nobody, that he rode for table scraps. Men in the bar would flirt with her; that was why the owner had hired her.

In time Carl saw that whenever anyone offered a hint about how an upcoming race might turn out, Christine seemed less fed up. She tried to look untouchable, but clearly she would pay attention if you said certain things. It became her reputation. If a rider or a trainer had something to say, something to tell her, she would listen. Carl, of course, had practically nothing to offer in this arena—not until Big Zip came along. After this, Carl felt as if he had some things to say to her. Big Zip gave him that.

Even right now, right this minute, after leaving Michael at the coffee shop, Carl couldn't say for certain that he loved Christine. He would have to admit that he longed for her attention. He wanted her to listen to him. Perhaps love arrived at times in this shape, in this category. Whenever he looked at her he would think, All right, I'm ready to talk. I want to talk about what I know for sure.

He opened the door to the bar and a ray of winter light shot right past him, went all the way to the counter. Michelle Branch played from the jukebox. Christine always looks in the direction of the door when it opens, he thought. Carl smiled at her. She bent forward, lifted a bottle of wine and when he shook his head, she reached for club soda. A couple of grooms from Tanya Nehi's barn inhabited one end of the counter. Geezers played cards at one of the tables; at another a pair of young couples split an iced bucket of beer. Carl sat at the spot where Christine had placed his glass of soda. She wiped her hands on a little towel she kept behind the counter. She stood and glanced down at Carl with both hands on her hips. She nodded. "How do," she said.

Carl thought about what he wanted to tell her. He said, "He's never going to let you go." He was not trying to scare her, but he did wish she'd appear worried, at least a little. Carl touched the edge of his soda glass. "Why did you want me to talk to him, Christine?"

"You're the jockey." Her lips barely seemed to move. Carl turned his shoulders, glanced at the room. He had a feeling of helplessness that he wanted to give in to. She said, "I wanted you to know he was out there. I didn't like the idea of lying to you."

He focused on the jukebox, the illuminated blue neon lights running along the frame. Without turning back, he said, "You could've lied to me. That would have been all right. I don't recall asking for complete honesty. Did I ask for that?"

"You want me to order a plate of—"

"No." He turned to face her again, then lowered his eyes, looked at the glass. "It's all right," he said. "Everything will remain the same."

"I want it to. I really do. I like winning."

"Well, hell yes," he said. "I'm glad tomorrow's a race day, aren't you?"

She nodded.

He closed his right hand, tapped his knuckles on the counter. "I owe you for the soda," he said.

Carl wanted to eat, but he waited until he was back in the apartment. He opened the kitchen cupboard; she had added to his tuna supply. Almost certainly, she possessed good intentions. This was what he ate and she simply wanted him to have more of it. Carl couldn't help but think of a pet-food section at a grocery store, however. The tins were neatly stacked. Each of them held a small portion of food. It was enough for a meal. Of course, Carl had learned this long ago. A squeeze of lemon, a few bits of ground pepper. He stood before the cupboard and the newly purchased tins of tuna and he couldn't help but think about his life on the whole. What he wanted. The way that he conducted himself. It all seemed very primitive. I ride horses, he thought. That's what I know, and when Christine and I talk it's really all I have to say. Nothing will be different tomorrow.

Carl wanted to avoid this onrush of despair. He closed his eyes for a moment, then opened them again and thought, All I need to do is hang on. Hold on. Ride my horses and then come back here and live with Christine. He thought, I knew it wouldn't last anyway. He closed the cupboard and opened it again. He took in a deep breath and exhaled. He stared at the tuna tins. *I am a tuna tin.*

Carl didn't want company and he didn't want her to see him this way. He was beginning to feel philosophical. In this apartment, he had tried to create a certain type of reality for himself. Now he had to face an additional reality, one that might wind up eliminating the one he wanted. He'd ridden in a dozen states and couldn't remember each racetrack anymore. Some, more than a few, had gone extinct. When you couldn't establish yourself in one place, you needed to move on to another, and when you did this you learned to tell yourself that the new place would be worth moving to because things could be different there. At the very least, you had to manifest the appearance and demeanor of a man who believed these things to be true. If you had been around long enough, your reputation might arrive just ahead of you and you'd need to show the local horsemen that you didn't carry your discouragements with you. You were only there to ride. Over the years, Carl had learned how to present himself this way. He hated this. It was dishonest, and it provided him with the greatest regret about his own life. He hadn't thought he'd need to call on this particular skill so early this year, in this particular year especially. Christine had told Carl that she and Michael were "walking through the ruins." In a way, even this meant they were still together.

Could he already be losing his focus? His touch? Spring had just begun. He had been riding in races for almost twenty-nine years. Lying awake that night with the lights off, his eyes open, he understood, perhaps for the first time, that he actually might have chosen the exact wrong profession for his life. Carl thought, I have always taken losing so badly. This alone might be the reason he was not, nor would be ever be, a top jockey. A top rider didn't care about losing, at least not in this way. It didn't make his heart sink. It didn't make him sometimes feel that everything would be lost. Losing just made a top rider more determined. It made him want everything that much more. But this had not been the case at all for Carl. It had just eaten at him, bit by bit, for the longest time. *How much of me is left?* He thought of the kitchen shelves in the apartment, the ones stacked with tuna tins.

Carl awakened without an alarm the next morning, as usual, and he turned to look over at Christine, though he couldn't see anything in the darkness of the room. He thought about reaching for her shoulder, waking her, but could not think of what to say if he did. He pulled himself quietly out of bed, walked to the bureau, took out socks, underwear, jeans, a long-sleeve t-shirt, and he dressed in the bathroom. He felt exhausted, looked down at his bare feet. He wanted to brush his teeth.

He showed up on time to work out the horses he had agreed to work out. He talked with the trainers of these horses afterward. The last horse Carl got on, a chestnut mare named Feeling So Pretty, had a rattling, uneven stride, as if the track itself were knee-deep in tin cans. Following the workout, Carl chatted with the trainer, Fredi Garcia, and he wondered if he should comment on the horse's unsoundness. Carl thought, Fredi knows this. We're talking about this horse's next race, but we are kidding ourselves. Even if it wins, we are kidding ourselves. I just don't understand it. Carl shook his head at one point while Fredi was talking about running the horse in a long-distance race next week, something at a mile and an eighth. "What is it?" Fredi said.

"Nothing."

"You okay?"

Carl rubbed his eyes with his fingers. "Yeah. My mind just drifted there for a second." Carl stuck his hands on his hips and stared at Fredi. "I'm listening."

Carl was having coffee with Christine later that morning and he broke away from discussing that afternoon's seventh race. "Have I ever mentioned a horse named Feeling So Pretty?" he said. "An old mare I get on for Fredi Garcia?"

Christine held a pen in her hand and had a notebook in her lap. She stopped writing in the notebook and looked up. She had her hair tied in a ponytail and the ponytail rested over one shoulder. Her face was scrubbed and her eyes were bright. "No, I don't think so," she said.

"Just some old head-banger," Carl said. His voice drifted. "Table scraps."

"And?"

"He wants to run her next week. I felt like saying 'Why don't you retire this goddamn heap? Call it quits before she breaks down and falls dead right on top of me.'"

Christine blinked at him. "Why didn't you?"

"Because then where would I be?"

"Well, I guess you wouldn't have to ride Feeling So Pretty anymore."

"Nobody will use a crack-up," he said.

They sat at the table in the quiet for a time. Christine sipped from her coffee mug. She closed the notebook, set it on the table. She placed the pen on top of it.

Carl said, "You got that right. I am not going to win a race today."

"Why don't you tell me what's bothering you?"

Carl glanced at the window. "It seems like you're a shrink sitting there like that with a pen and a pad and everything."

"You are living here with me. I'm not your fucking secretary, Carl."

"It's Michael," he said, almost immediately. "You know that."

"I told you, he and I...drifted apart."

"Apart," he said. She had lowered her head. He waited until she looked his way. Carl said, "It's all right, Christine. I have a past, too. Every time I want to see you I don't always see you." His voice lost some of it firmness. What he said was not true. He suspected they both knew it. "I don't want to think about what I don't have. Wanting too much is sad. Being satisfied is sad, too." He cut his right hand into the air. "I'm trying to get it right there in between." He smiled and hoped she was watching him. "But it's tough."

"I know."

"It's hard to stay on a winning streak. You have to forget practically everything."

"Maybe we ought to get you hypnotized."

"I tried that once, I think," he said. He wanted to say, I think I've tried just about everything. But he didn't want her to hear as much. He didn't want her to hear these particular words. "Don't get carried away with your gambling, Christine," he said. "Don't think that any of this is easy." She regarded him in a patient way. "I know what you have been through."

"What are you trying to tell me?" she said.

"I feel a little slump coming on. Maybe you better hang on to your money for a little bit."

"Are you trying to punish me or something, Carl?"

"No." He shook his head at this. "Not at all."

8.

Carl began to lose something in his race riding. Speed horses invariably faded, pace-stalkers refused to change gears, closers made half-hearted charges. In the feature race on one sunny Sunday afternoon, he lost his whip fifty yards from the finish. He showed it to his horse, held the whip forward so the horse could see the possibility of it. He brought his arm back to strike the horse's flank one time and the thing flew away like it was hit by a warlock's curse. The horse, a bony three-year-old named Muttering, had a half-length lead when this happened and without the whip the horse's ears went up and it went to loafing, got caught just a few strides from the finish. The horse had been winless in eleven straight races prior to this. His trainer waited to talk with Carl after the race, but when Carl began to walk in her direction, she turned and strode away from him. Carl didn't know if Christine had wagered on this horse; he certainly hadn't liked their chances going into the race.

When he arrived home from work that afternoon, Carl found a racing program on the stand on his side of the bed.

The program came from that day's races at Summit and it lay open to the last race on the card, a race he hadn't been in. He could imagine Michael lying on this bed, looking at the program while listening to a live call of the race on the internet. She might have been lying there with him. They might have talked about their future once old Carl Arvo stepped aside. The bed had been neatly made; the program was the one thing he hadn't expected to see in the bedroom. Someone wanted him to see it. Maybe her. She had tried so hard to be clear with him all along. Carl stood in the bedroom for a minute and then he grabbed the program from the nightstand, folded it twice, took it out to the kitchen and stuffed it in the trash.

A few days after this, Carl and Christine sat at the little kitchen table and he had gone over a few of the day's races with her when he began to flex his hands. She had not written much in her notebook during that morning's session, but she had not closed the notebook, nor had she set down the pen. Carl thought these to be hopeful signs. He said, "You know, I have dropped a whip in a race before last week. It's happened before." They had not talked about the whip-dropping incident, but Christine did not look surprised.

"Oh?"

"Sure, a couple of years back, in a race at Balmoral. Another time at The Woodlands. It's happened any number of times."

Christine brushed at something on her forehead and held the pen over the pad. "Want me to make a list?"

"No," he said. "I do not."

"Okay. Are you telling me not to worry?"

"I'm telling myself not to, I guess."

"Are you worried, Carl?"

He exhaled. "I don't know if worried is the right word for it." Carl watched her for a moment. "What I am struggling with now I have struggled with for a while." He forced a grin and said, "A long time. I think the condition is what doctors call mediocrity." He shrugged. "It comes and goes." The room turned quiet. He thought Christine might make a joke, but she didn't. Carl felt bothered by this. "You're not winning at the windows."

"I'm learning how things work," she said. "I'm ahead for the spring. How many people can say that?"

"Christine."

"What?"

"Have you spoken to Michael in a while?"

She paused, looked down at the pad.

He knew the answer.

She said, "Look, he stops by the Seven Seas. I've told you that. There's nothing I can do about it."

"Michael is the reason I am in a slump," he said.

"No, he's not," Christine said. "That's not true at all. I told you about him before you moved in here. Didn't I? Say it."

"You did."

"I don't understand how you can blame your slide on that."

Carl didn't want to argue. He was not afraid to argue with her, but he didn't want to. *Slide.* He did not care for that word. "I created a little world where I was a good rider and I had everything I needed. This apartment. You. Endless supply of Starkist." He waved his arm in the direction of the cupboard. He felt like making a joke about Mrs. Lovain. Even she keeps her blinds open for me...she did a little dance in the kitchen last week. He smiled at Christine, but it didn't feel good.

She slapped then pen on the open notebook at this. "You are talking like everything is over. What's gotten into you?"

"What are you going to do about Michael?" he said.

Christine placed the notebook atop the table. "I don't know."

"Where does he sit?"

"What?"

"When he's at the bar, where does he sit?"

"He sits at the counter with all the other horse guys. I talk to him. I mean, there he is. I think he's trying, you know? Why shouldn't I listen? Why shouldn't I let him feel better now? He hates himself. It's hard to sit by..."

"Any man sitting in my chair would feel like he was in competition with Michael."

"But that's not why you moved in, Carl."

Carl hoped they wouldn't get into a discussion about dating other people, that she would say something like, *You can see whoever you want* and so forth.

"Is it?" she said.

"You seemed like someone I could talk to."

"Yeah, I like this part, too," she said. "Look, you want to tell me some more about today's races or what?"

Carl drew in a breath, then exhaled again. "I'll try."

At the end of that week, late on Saturday afternoon, Carl stretched out on the bed where he and Christine slept. He had been home from the races for just a few minutes. One more winless day there. Inside the pocket of his shirt, his cell rang. When he brought the phone above his eyes, he saw the number was local, the name of the caller unknown. Carl suspected a trainer, someone new to town.

Carl said hello and the voice on the other end said, "Carl Arvo?"

The voice seemed familiar. A male's voice younger than his own. He thought, Teddy? My son? "Yes?" he said.

"Michael Fleming here. Carl, how are you?"

Carl stared at the ceiling. He did not respond.

"I know you are there," Michael said. "I can see the word bubble over your head right now. It's saying 'Of all the fucking people…'"

"That's close."

"I do have that effect."

"I am here," Carl said. "What can I do for you?"

"Well, it's been three weeks, almost a month."

"And?"

"We said a month. We talked about that, remember?"

Carl's throat went dry and he forced himself to swallow. "A month? You couldn't go a couple of days without talking to her."

"That wasn't the deal," Michael said. "What you said was that she couldn't complain to you about me. I know she hasn't done that."

"You got the apartment under surveillance?"

"I asked her not to complain. I said, 'Look, if you complain, he isn't going to give me a horse.'"

"What did she say to that?"

"She understood, I guess."

"How do you know that, Michael?"

"She wants me back. All of this is because of that."

"Yeah, but here we are…What does she say when she talks about me?"

"What?"

Carl placed his free hand on the center of his chest. "I'm not going to give you any horse unless you answer the question I just asked you."

Michael said, "This is crazy. I'm not going to get into that."

"I'm hanging up in three seconds."

More than three seconds elapsed. Carl did not close his phone.

"She doesn't complain about you, if that's what you're asking. It's not like she has to carry the weight of you on her shoulders or anything."

"That's right."

"What's that?"

"Christine's not a complainer, anyway. You ought to know that by now."

"These were your conditions," Michael said.

"I wish she did complain. It would make things a lot easier, you know?" Carl considered things for a time. "You're a real stupid little fucker, you know that, Michael?"

Michael did not respond, not immediately. When he did, he said, "Why haven't you won a race this week? What's wrong with your riding anyway? You started off the meet pretty good, sport."

Carl thought of Teddy again, about what Teddy might say about his father, if he was ever asked. *He just wants to ride, that's all.* "I'm doing all right."

"What were you up to on Green Ripper yesterday? You sent it to the front, then took it back."

"I know what happened. Bet on it the next time it runs," Carl said. "There'll be a different jockey on him. You'll make a fortune. There. There's your inside information for the month. How's that?"

"I already know this," Michael said. "I'm not blind. How does it qualify as inside info if I already know it?"

Carl pulled the phone away from his face. He decided to concentrate on his own breathing. He brought the phone back to his cheek and said, "Everybody knows everything. Haven't you been paying attention at all?" He closed the phone, pitched it over to Christine's side of the bed.

Later that afternoon Carl awakened from a restless sleep. He felt full of aches. His cell kept ringing. He carefully lifted the phone, looked at the number first, saw it was an unfamiliar area code. The sound of Michael Fleming's voice was still in his ears. Carl waited. He thought, This might be one of mine. A wife or a son or a daughter. An unhappy voice. It was pointless to avoid it. He opened the phone, and into it, said, "Hello."

On the end of the line, a man's voice said, "I am looking for Carl Arvo."

"You found him," Carl said.

"Hello, Carl, how are you?" The man's voice was clear and strong.

"Fine. Good."

"Carl, my name is Tom Westfeld." Seconds passed.

"Oh…Tom Westfeld. That name is familiar to me."

"I'm sure it is."

"Well, Tom Westfeld," Carl said.

"Yes."

"Well, well."

"I phoned the racing office at Summit Park and asked them for the number of your agent. The secretary said he didn't think you had an agent."

"No," he said. "I don't."

"You need an agent, if you don't mind me saying as much."

Carl touched his fingers to his eyebrows. "You're the guy who bought Big Zip," he said. He closed his eyes. He wished he hadn't said this aloud.

"That's right."

Carl kept his eyes closed. "Well, it's nice to talk to you, Tom."

"I'm glad I found you, Carl. Do you have a minute or two to talk with me?"

"Of course," Carl said.

"I'm sure you know BZ is on something of a losing streak out here in California. Since the first day we brought him out here, the pattern has been the same. He works out well in the mornings. When I say he works out well, I mean there isn't a horse on the grounds that can keep up with him. I have twenty-three horses of my own stabled at Balboa Park. They have cost me millions. And BZ is faster than each and every one of them. The problem is when he races in the afternoons. In his races, he breaks sharply, but as soon as another horse gets near him, he loses his focus. He shuts it all down. We have tried various things with him. Blinkers, D-bit, shadow roll. We have tried any number of riders. He raced last in the Ancient Title. I had Victor Herrera in the saddle, for heaven's sake. He won the Eclipse last year as best jockey in the nation."

Carl said, "I know who he is."

"These riders out here keep telling me the same thing. They keep telling me this horse can't finish a race. Imagine that, these riders…my trainer, Henry Forrest, he says that he isn't out of ideas. But the fact is that BZ put up better speed numbers last fall when you were on him. I've seen tapes of those races and I liked how handled yourself. Confidence. You ride him like you didn't have any question…this is what we need. It's what we have to have.

"Now, Henry has objected to this, but in the end, I am the boss, this is my stable. What I want to do is fly you out here and have you get on BZ a couple of mornings. Get used to how he feels, tell us if he's missing anything. I want you to ride him in the San Diego Handicap on Saturday. Of course, I will pay for your flight and your hotel…Balboa Park is a wonderful place. Have you ridden out here before?"

"No," Carl said.

"I'd like to fly you out here on Wednesday—this Wednesday. I'll have a man pick you up at the airport. You can work out the horse for us on Thursday and Friday. Get your license. Then the race is on Saturday. Does this sound all right to you, Carl? Can you find the time to come out here and help us? I know you want to see this horse do well. On top of your expenses and ten percent of the purse, I'll pay you five thousand dollars."

Carl said, "I never thought I'd get the chance to ride that horse again. I put it out of my mind. I just try to appreciate what I have, you know?"

"Great," Tom Westfeld said. "I'm going to have my secretary call you tomorrow and you all work out the flight and everything else. On Monday, she'll overnight you DVDs that have all the of horse's races out here. Call my office…here's the number…give her your address. Her name is Wilma. Watch these tapes, will you, please? See if you see anything at all that can help us. I will look for you on Thursday morning at our Balboa Park barn. I'll introduce you to Henry. Now, he is a bit crusty…Carl, I'm sure you're used to trainers by now."

"Most of them."

Tom Westfeld gave a quick laugh. "Good. See you soon," he said.

Carl laid his arms flat on the bed covers. He held the cell phone in his right fist. Did I say yes? he thought. Did this guy even ask? Men like that knew you would not, you could not say no. Because what they were talking about was all they believed in. They understood that you would never say no because they themselves could never say no. You didn't need to say yes. We don't look out at an ocean here, Carl thought. This is Ohio. That't not lost on anyone.

His thoughts moved quickly. He brought the phone to his eyes, rolled down his list of contacts until he came to Christine, then touched the dial. When she answered, she said, "Carl?" There were voices, music in the background. Saturday evening. Two-for-one drinks till nine.

"Can you grab a few minutes?" he said.

"I can't. Not right now. No way."

"I want to talk with you."

"Everything okay?"

"No. Well, yes."

"Come on down here. Sit at the counter. You can talk to me there."

Would Michael be there? The news he had he didn't want anyone else to hear. He wanted to explain all of the details.

"Carl?"

"Call me when you're on a break."

"Sure," she said. "No worries."

She phoned more than an hour later. By this time, Carl was into the wine with the bicycles on the label. Half a bottle's worth. The drinking hit him in a forceful way.

"So, what is it?" she said. "Tell me."

"Where are you?"

"Back office. I asked if I could use it for a few minutes. You okay?"

"I've had half a bottle of wine," he said.

"Oh shit," she said. "You're on five tomorrow."

"Christine, you know that I am in love with you. You know that, don't you?"

"Is that what you wanted to tell me?"

He wanted to tell her the truth. "No."

"I guess I suspected as much," she said.

"The guy who owns Big Zip wants me to fly out there on Wednesday night. Do morning workouts, then ride the horse in the San Diego Handicap on Saturday."

"Unreal," she said. A pause followed. He wished he had given her the news when they were together. He could only picture her face. "That's kind of fantastic."

"I know. I've been sitting here, thinking about it, you know? This is not entirely unprecedented, however. Canonero II, that horse from Venezuela who won the Triple Crown in '70 or '71, he was bought by the King Ranch after that but they couldn't win a race with him. Then they finally brought back Gustavo Avila, the guy who won the Derby and Preakness on him. Avila rode Canonero in the Discovery Handicap. They set a world record for a mile and an eighth. And old Johnnie Oldham, nothing but a biscuit-and-gravy man, rode Rockhill Native every race. That horse was a two-year-old champion. There are certain guys who fit certain horses. Only those guys won on those horses."

"Would this be like the biggest thing in your life—if you can win it?"

"I want you to go with me," he said. "The guy said they'd fly my woman and me out to California first class."

A pause followed. Faintly, he could hear the jukebox. Springsteen. Maybe "The Rising." She said, "No. I don't think so." Then, "That's four days' work. No, I can't do that."

"Ever been to California?"

"California will be there for me, Carl."

"This is the biggest thing that's happened to me in a while," he said.

"We've been together a month. A month and some change," she said. "Big Zip is your deal."

"I knew I could talk you into letting me move in with you." He pictured the office. A cluttered desk. Cases of booze stacked in a corner. A poster for *Major League* on the wall. A Browns schedule from two years back, when they made the playoffs. Cleveland forever.

She said, "You did, huh?"

"As soon as I leave town, your ex is going to show up at your front door."

"Let's talk about this tomorrow."

"Tell me now," he said. "Part of it, anyway. I'm getting bored with this feeling of euphoria."

"I want to honor the commitment I made to you," she said. "But the longer it goes on, the more difficult this is probably going to be. Look at you; you're in a slump now. This is supposed to be the best season…Things are getting complicated. Going out to California to ride that horse is a good thing. You agree to it pretty quick?"

"He didn't have to ask."

"Some people are that way," she said in a quieter voice.

"I'd rather stay here with you."

"Enough of that."

"What? You are super wonder fucking woman? Your twat is that delicious?"

"I am going to hang up on you."

"Can we start over again?"

"Night," she said.

The line went dead.

He said, "Yep. She said she would."

9.

The following morning, once workouts had concluded, he returned to the apartment and they had coffee together. This was a Sunday morning, a cloudy and cold one and Carl's arms and legs were like clay. It felt as if he had already lost everything. He said, "Navajo Canyon, that small gray filly I'm on in the second…she doesn't like to be whipped at all. I learned this about her last time I rode her. We finished mid-pack in a maiden claimer, what, nine days ago?"

"Right," Christine said. "That was a Friday."

"The trainer, Jose Able, he's a nice guy who ought to be selling Vitamin Water or some goddamn thing. Last time, he told me that when it was time for us to make our move, I needed to show her the whip, then get to sticking her. When I showed her the whip, she accelerated. When I hit her with the thing, she just flattened out. I think she was telling me she understood how it all worked. Jose has her back in the same kind of race today. I am going to ignore his instructions. She ought to go forward a few lengths."

"Think she'll get a piece?" She made notes as she spoke.

Carl waited until she looked up at him. "I'd be surprised if she didn't," he said.

Christine nodded.

"I thought we'd catch the six o'clock to San Diego on Wednesday afternoon," he said. "Have dinner on the plane. Lobster or steak." He smiled, which he wanted her to see.

"How am I going to bet *that* race?" she said.

With your hands and your pocketbook, Carl felt like joking. Suddenly, he felt a great many things, but none of these feelings were actually helpful. He was pleased that Christine appeared to be in a thoughtful frame of mind.

"You are going to call me on Saturday morning, right?" her voice said. There was a pleasant, false touch of urgency.

Carl said, "What do I know about riding in California?"

"It's Big Zip. What else do you need to know?"

Carl dropped his head, let his shoulders sag. "That's all it takes? Well, hell."

"Tell me what you think…right this second."

"Del Mar has an artificial surface. I rode on artificial at Turfway in northern Kentucky a couple of seasons ago. The track surface there is made of little bits of carpet and tiny bits of rubber. The horses don't make any sound when they run. You can't hear their hoofbeats. Weird. They say it's safer than dirt." Carl couldn't read her expression. "Don't do anything stupid, okay, Christine? Like bet all the money you've already made. Big Zip has been on a losing streak out there and it's probably for one reason and one reason alone. Those horses out there are just a hell of a lot faster. Asking me to go out there and change all that is an act of desperation. The guy who owns the horse could have said as much."

"All you're doing now is protecting yourself against disappointment."

"I guess so."

"This could be the start of something great," she said.

"I hope it is. I really do."

"It'll be a good trip. I already have a positive vibe about it."

"Will everything be different when I get back?" Carl hadn't wanted to ask the question. It was one more thing to think about, one more thing to throw him off.

"This will be your place," she said. "You don't have to worry about where you'll be living. If that's what you mean."

"And you will be here?"

"Yes. Of course. I'll be here on Sunday. Is that when you get back?"

"Where does Michael live?" Carl said. "I don't think I've ever asked you that."

"He has an apartment on the east end of St. Clair Avenue. It's a sublet. He pays by the month."

Carl would lose Christine to Michael. He had known this for as long as he could care to admit. Little would be proved by getting angry with her. He might as well pack up his boxes and head for the next place. Charles Town. Mountaineer. Right this second, he hoped that she could read his mind. He said, "I might just go out there and win on that goddamn horse. Upset of the century."

Christine nodded at this. There was an informed look to her expression.

"Anyway, you know better than to bet everything," he said.

Navajo Canyon, Carl's best chance to win a race that afternoon, finished a faraway second to a first-time starter named Exemplary. Carl tried hard and rode capably on his remaining mounts, but he couldn't keep his mind clear. There'd been a time when losing had brought clarity to his thinking. When he was younger, losing had meant he'd made poor choices with his life. It suggested he had significant shortcomings. He remembered having long talks about losing with his first wife, Kelly, while they were still married. They did this for good reason. They were broke and boom-boom-boom had three children. Kelly talked about losing too much. He began to blame her for his losing, even though he already knew losing was always going to be a big part of this.

Carl had spoken with Kelly on the phone last Christmas. She'd remarried years ago and now worked in the human resources office at the University of Akron. Their kids had turned into adults; both daughters lived in Akron, had married men from there. They were close to their mother. At one point during their talk last Christmas, Kelly told Carl each girl wanted to start a family soon. Are you ready to be a grandfather, Carl? Kelly had said. Sure, of course, Carl said right away. Kelly didn't go on to tease him about riding racehorses and being a grandfather. This almost certainly would be the case. Their son, Teddy, had struck out on his own, and from what Carl had gathered, Teddy liked to sell things. He made good money at it. Carl and Kelly's kids were average-sized, like their mother. Carl talked to everyone twice a year, around Christmas and on individual birthdays. He didn't know about their problems. He wanted to be helpful to his wives and children, but he supposed the only way of doing that was through money. They probably had more than he did, anyway. Everyone was polite.

Alycia, Carl's second wife, had once said to him, You will always win just enough to believe you have done the right thing with your life. She had said this after a fight, not during one.

At the time, Carl thought this was an overly dramatic offering. Carl had talked to her this past Christmas, like he always did. She and Carl, like Carl and Kelly, had an unspoken rule about bringing up the past. Carl, for whatever reason, had felt like reminding her of that line, though he didn't want to revive any dead and buried issues. He simply wanted to tell her that she had been correct. It hadn't changed anything when she'd said it for the first time and it certainly would not change anything now. That was how right she had been. He simply wanted to tell her he wanted more these days. He thought she might like to hear that. But none of this would matter to Alycia.

She had remarried too and now lived in Erie, Pennsylvania. Her Facebook posts suggested she liked taking her camera to the lake. Alycia was tall and blond and still slim. Her husband was a big man with a chiseled face. He looked like Chuck Woollery. In practically all of her Facebook photos, Alycia was smiling, with Chuck embracing her in many of them. Carl hoped there was not a falseness to this, that this wasn't simply because the camera was on them. Carl knew his time with Alycia had come and gone. He had missed out with her. He could stand it. But, he was strong enough to still wonder about it.

On Monday evening Carl packed a suitcase for his trip to San Diego. He had moved in with two different suitcases, one a large vinyl case with an endless number of zippers and pockets, and in this he kept clothes—jeans, western shirts—he hadn't worn in a while but for some reason couldn't part with. In there, too, were old racing programs and some win photos from when he first started out as a rider. He hadn't looked at them in years. He knew he wouldn't use the case for anything else. There weren't going to be any vacations to the Bahamas. That was all right; the realization of this had barely bothered him at all.

The other case he had was smaller, for overnight trips. It had a retractable aluminum handle on one end and wheels at the other. He had bought this perhaps a half-dozen years ago, perhaps even longer, when he decided the larger case would only be used to store things he wanted to hang on to. He bought the smaller case—and he remembered this idea specifically now—because it might be useful if someone wanted to fly him in for a certain race. When he bought the smaller case, he still had not given up on the idea this might happen. He lived with Christine and now another thing he had fantasized about was actually going to happen. He could never have predicted the exact circumstances. He never thought he would ride at a place like Balboa Park; he'd only allowed himself to hope for a ride at Philly Park or one of the tracks in Jersey.

Carl had stored both cases in a closet in the bedroom he shared with Christine. The closet door was always open because Bo's litter box was in there. When he brought out the smaller case, it felt light. In fact, when he unzipped the front flap, he saw the case was empty. He set the empty case on the bed and supposed that in the end he was still something of a fool, nothing more than a superstitious creature. He had left it empty for a reason. Carl decided to leave the opened case on the bed with the hope that Bo might appear and climb into it. Cats liked doing things like this. Carl left the bedroom and when he returned after messing around on his computer for an hour, he saw the case was still empty. Carl kept his eyes on the case and tried to remember the last time he had seen Bo. On occasion the cat had walked out to the kitchen area while Carl ate a tin of tuna and worked at his computer. Carl looked under the bed. Nothing, no shining cat eyes looking back. He walked to the closet again because he realized something. When he had been in there a few minutes ago, he hadn't had to step around the litter box. He looked again in the closet and discovered the box was gone. There was nothing wrong with Bo; Christine would have said something. He stepped out of the closet and eyed the empty suitcase on the bed. In a while, he began to pack.

II.

1.

Carl had bought an airplane ticket for Christine. He'd ordered this with Tom Westfeld's secretary, asked her to deduct the price of the seat from the five grand Westfeld promised him. Carl printed out the tickets and the boarding passes. He placed Christine's on the kitchen table on Tuesday morning as they had coffee together. He said, "Just cash it in if you don't want to go. Bet it on something fast."

That afternoon, she had been gone for an hour when a FedEx delivery man brought a package to the door, a package from La Jolla, California. Carl felt sheepish about having sold his flat-screen, although Christine's TV did have a DVD player. Everything would have been so much clearer on the flat-screen. Carl watched Big Zip's California races on her TV. He had already seen these races at the Summit OTB parlor and in every one the story had more or less been the same. Big Zip would fight for the early lead. A couple of times, the horse would get a daylight advantage as the field raced for the far turn, but then couldn't hold it. Big Zip was a very fast horse, and getting the lead early was important to him. You couldn't change anything about that at all.

When Carl had ridden him, the wins at Summit had been easy ones and Carl hadn't learned much about the horse in them. Carl had then ridden Big Zip in the Milwaukee Avenue Handicap in Chicago, and in that race, Big Zip broke a step slow and found himself in a speed duel with two other horses. The horse ran well, had its ears pricked, which was always the key clue with a speed horse. But they couldn't shake free of the others and Carl brought out the stick, waved it in Big Zip's periphery. Carl struck the horse on the flank with the whip turning for home and Big Zip responded, got a half-length in front. When Carl whipped the horse again, Big Zip's ears flattened and he eased himself. Carl loosened the reins and lunged forward in the saddle, kept the whip out of sight. Big Zip found a second wind late in the race and was gaining again on the two horses that had passed them in mid-stretch.

No doubt, this race had been viewed by Westfeld and his bunch over and over. They probably had their own theories as to how the horse responded to the whip. In the races in California, Big Zip didn't appear to respond to the whip at all. If anything, the horse seemed to resent it. No matter who rode Big Zip, be it Baze or Jenkins or Herrera, as soon as the rider got busy with the stick, the horse stopped running. Carl wound up with a little knot in his stomach. Did he know something a few of best jockeys in the world had missed? He thought, Look, it's pretty simple, guys. Show him the whip at the right moment. Use it one time and one time only. Carl watched the California races over and over. That will be me, he thought. Even if he won out there, he wanted to ride in Cleveland all spring and summer long. His business would be incredible.

Carl watched the horse's first race in California a half-dozen times. This was the seven-furlong Malibu Stakes where Big Zip wound up finishing tenth in a twelve-horse field. The race was unremarkable in this way. Carl recalled standing in the OTB parlor, watching it. He'd always felt the California horses would be too much for Big Zip. He had watched the race, and as the horse faded he felt something about his own fortunes—that even though this horse had created good business for Carl the good business was not going to last. He needed to go ahead and reach for something he otherwise wouldn't be likely to have.

Carl ejected the DVD and went to bed early. He lay in bed and at one point even said aloud, "Enough." It simply wasn't easy. The following afternoon, as he waited at the flight gate, Carl did not expect to see Christine. He had mixed emotions about the possibility of seeing her. If she showed, the trip would be about them, not the race. There would be the slightest change to his focus. But he knew she wouldn't show and he told himself it was for the best. He boarded the plane alone, found his place in first class. He stretched out there. He had an aisle seat and the window seat next to him was empty. His eyes were closed when the plane left the ground.

He slept, and when he awakened, a slender young man in dark blue trousers, a white shirt and a dark blue vest stood before him. The man in the blue vest had his hands folded in front of him like someone making a wish. Carl decided to reach up and shake hands with him.

"Oh," the man said.

Carl said, "My first time in first class." The headrest was tilted back, the footrest extended. "Feels like I'm on a raft."

The man in the vest had thin black hair combed neatly to one side. His arms were tan and he wore a watch with a brown leather band. "We're serving dinner now," he said. "Tonight's choices are—"

Carl waved at him. "No, no," he said. "I'm riding in the San Diego Handicap on Saturday."

The man seemed to understand. "Can I bring you anything else? We have fruit. Strawberries, grapes. We have wine. I can bring you a hot towel, if you like."

"The towel will be good later," Carl said. Beyond the window, past the empty seat,the sky had filled with a soft, mauve-colored light. "Where are we now? What do you say your name is?"

"My name is Lucas," he said.

Carl rubbed at his mouth. "Where are we now, Lucas?"

"Um, Illinois, I think. Somewhere over Illinois."

"I'm riding a horse named Big Zip," Carl said. "Ever heard of him?" The man shook his head, though only slightly. Carl said, "Do you have any frozen grapes? I ask because I rode one summer at Hazel Park, down there in Michigan." He pointed at a section of aisle carpeting with his left hand. "Half of us were starving just to make riding weight, you know. Hotter than Satan's peter down there that summer. So, what the jocks'-room manager used to do was set out bowls of frozen grapes after every race. You could eat just three or four of them, but you would feel revived. I didn't have a bad summer at all." He said this with a laugh. "After Hazel, I went to Atlantic City for the fall. I wound up sleeping on park benches there. But the thing is ever since then I have preferred frozen grapes to cool ones or room-temperature ones. Every time I eat a chilled grape, I wished it was a frozen one."

"I could try to work out something—"

"Oh, no," Carl said. "Don't worry about that at all, Lucas. I do think I will take that towel in about an hour, though. Till then I think I will just lie here."

Lucas held his hands together and gave a quick bow. Carl appreciated this. He turned his head to the empty window seat again and thought how strange it might have been had Christine decided to join him on this trip. Flying was quite intimate. There was no telling what they might have started to get into. Carl felt ready to ride now. He wanted to see Big Zip and he wanted to feel this fast horse under him again. On Saturday, he would get Big Zip away from the gate quick, make the lead and keep the horse a few paths out from the rail. Big Zip didn't like having anything in front of him and in Cleveland the horse had been fast enough to keep things just this way. Carl wanted to win the San Diego Handicap, and, during some moments every day since he'd gotten the call from Tom Westfeld, he had allowed himself to imagine winning it. He saw the finish, then he imagined easing upward in the saddle for the gallop out. He wouldn't want to wave his fist in the air like some excited riders would after a big win. He wouldn't want to wave his whip in the air at God, or make a sign of the cross. He would save that for a time in his life when he wound up alone in some god-forsaken motel room, by himself, and couldn't find anything else to hang on to. He would tell himself, All right, I won the freaking San Diego Handicap. No matter what happened this weekend, and no matter what happened with Christine for the rest of the spring, one day Carl would find himself in another motel room, trying to figure out what he ought to do next. Because this was exactly what was going to happen. Ronnie Franklin, a nobody, a seventeen-year-old kid off the streets, became the regular rider for Spectacular Bid, one of the greatest horses of the twentieth century. Franklin got fired after his lousy ride caused Spectacular Bid to lose the Belmont Stakes. He wound up working in a car wash. Gustavo Avila would only be remembered because of Canonero. The same held true for Oldham and Rockhill Native. When these horses finished racing, their riders just disappeared. Carl could win the San Diego 'Cap, and he might even become the regular rider for Big Zip again. Fly out here any time the horse ran. At forty-five years old, Carl wouldn't suddenly become a rare or a dazzling talent. His circuit had been established long ago. He would fly back to Cleveland or East St. Louis or Chester, West Virginia, after each race aboard Big Zip. The trajectory of his life would never change much. This had been the whole reason he wanted to live with Christine.

He tried to no longer think of her. He did imagine how things would be when he returned to Summit Park, how his business there would be affected depending on the outcome of the San Diego Handicap. If Big Zip won, of course, that would mean even more rides for Carl at home. He thought about Ilya Kamanakov and what Tom Westfeld had said about having an agent. Ilya had, in fact, taken on Guillermo Milord as his journeyman, but that probably was just a handshake deal. Nothing a better offer couldn't cure. Even if Big Zip finished up the track, a big stable at a major racetrack had still asked for Carl's services. That should be used to his advantage. He just needed to ride his best out here. He needed to show everyone that he could handle himself in the bright sunshine in front of a big Saturday afternoon crowd.

He was flying west, the clock was moving forward and backward at the same time. It remained early evening. When Lucas brought a small tray that held a white, warm towel, he held it out to Carl with a pair of tongs. Carl took the towel without thinking, immediately draped it over his face. This stung, but just for a second. In a moment, he made an okay sign with his right hand because he thought Lucas might be standing there, watching. While Carl had the towel on his face, the pilot came on the speaker, announced that Lindbergh Field, the San Diego International Airport, was just two hundred miles away.

A short blond man in a baseball cap met Carl at the airport. The man had lobster-colored skin and held up a yellow legal pad. On the first sheet, written in red marker, was RVO. The man stuck the pad under his arm and Carl shook hands with him. After that, the man, who smelled strongly of cigarette smoke, said, "Tab." He had weirdly blank blue eyes and odd-looking lips, like nightcrawlers. They walked through the main terminal together without a word until they hit the warm air outside. The night sky appeared plum-colored above and silver-like at the horizon. They found Tab's ivory SUV Explorer on the ground floor of the short-term lot. Tab paid the parking fee, then began to follow the exit arrows. He said, "You're staying at the Lemon Grove Hotel, a mile and a half from the track." He guided them into the high-speed lane. "I'll come by tomorrow morning to get you at five a.m."

"Five a.m. your time?" Carl felt his cheeks warm after this.

"Right," Tab said. Carl thought of what Tab was going to say next. If not our time, then what fucking time do you want it to be?

Carl tried to save it. "I'll get to sleep in a little," he said.

"Good," Tab said, for some reason.

It didn't matter what he said, Carl had expected this type of treatment. He was a nobody and he'd been called out here to figure out a horse that had stymied a world-class outfit for months. "What is Big Zip going to do tomorrow?"

"Henry Forrest will talk to you about that."

They barreled south to the interstate and to Carl's right were silhouettes of palm trees. They were deep green against the purple sky. "The ocean's over there, huh?" Carl said, nodding at the window on Tab's side.

Tab laughed in a short, unpleasant way. "Yeah, it sure is." Then he sighed. "Hey, man, take out your cell and key in my phone number. That way, you can call me if something comes up."

Carl tapped numerals in the order Tab had said them. This hardly mattered. Carl had Tom Westfeld's cell. This possibly had just dawned on Tab. "What might come up?" Carl said.

Tab laughed. "Maybe you'll get homesick."

"You ever been to Ohio?" Carl said.

Tab didn't laugh, and Carl didn't feel like laughing, either.

The hotel digs were impressive—a living-room area with an L-shaped, maroon leather couch in one corner, a TV set and mini-bar in another. The bedroom had a TV too, plus a trampoline-sized bed. Carl saw new packages in a closet—a white robe, white slippers—and he put them on. He went to the bedroom's mini-fridge to check on its supplies. Airline bottles of liquor and wine, bottles of beer, packages of gourmet cookies and crackers. A tight little row of oranges and mangoes on the door's top shelf. Inside, near the top, sat two full ice trays. Carl walked over to the bedside phone, touched 7 for room service, and asked that a bunch of grapes be sent up.

"Thank you," he said into the phone.

The hem of the robe fell to the tops of his feet. The slippers were cottony and soft. He felt like taking a picture of himself with his phone and emailing it to Christine. Subject line: Lucky Life. What happened, though, was that he went to the bed, lifted the remote from its little U-shaped plastic stand, and turned on the TV set. He eased down the sound and waited for the grapes to be delivered. What had he said to Tab? Ever been to Ohio? Carl had believed, for the longest time, that it was a fool's work to try and understand how much you loved or hated your own place in life. If things were going well, you stayed in the same spot, and when they weren't, you moved along. Being alive was not difficult in this way. Carl had just made a little joke about Ohio because he was trying to fit in out here, if just for a second or two.

He felt like calling Christine right now and saying to her, Honestly, do you hate Cleveland? But the sound of her voice would break his concentration. He remembered something she'd said when he'd first proposed living with her. She'd said, Won't I break your concentration? At the time, Carl had known he wanted to talk about the horses he rode. He'd known he wouldn't sound angry. He wouldn't sound bitter. He would look across the little kitchen table and there would be Christine, and he wouldn't have to convince himself things had not turned out badly in his life. He would understand they had not.

Of course, he couldn't climb onto the back of Big Zip and expect to win a race with all of these thoughts going on. Bitterness, this was always close at hand. It was always nearby. It followed him down the street, it lurked outside, in both the sunlight and the shadows. Big Zip had brought winning back into Carl's life, if only for a short time. Was Carl born so he could ride this horse? He thought of Christine again, wanted to call her and tell her he was wondering about this exact thing. It would surprise her to hear him talk this way. It would probably just sound as if he had already gotten carried away. It wouldn't mean she ought to bet on the horse on Saturday. He could call her and tell her what he was thinking because she knew how to separate these things.

There came a knock on the door of his room and when he opened it, a young, dark-haired man stood just beyond a rolling cart covered in a white tablecloth. The man wore a black vest, white shirt, and black trousers. Carl stood away from the door and the man wheeled in the cart. Atop a silver plate sat a sterling silver bowl with a heavy silver lid and a silver handle on top the size and shape of a half dollar. The man nodded to Carl and Carl held out his hand for the bill and a pen. "Are you taken care of on this?" Carl said. The man stood with his hands out to accept the pen and bill. He shook his head and Carl said, "Hang on." Carl walked over to the closet, took his pants from the floor, rooted in a pocket and found a twenty. "Here," Carl said, as he stepped in the direction of the man. "Thank you," Carl said. "Goodbye."

Carl guided the rolling cart close to the mini-fridge. He opened the door to that, took out an ice tray. He took a few grapes, five to be exact, and set them in the freezer area. He placed them apart from one another, as if this was a necessary part of it. He would have them on his way out tomorrow morning. He would recall that it had been as hot as hell that one summer at Hazel Park.

2.

Balboa Park racetrack stood across the highway from El Cajon Beach and the Pacific Ocean. Henry Forrest stabled his horses in one of the three dozen rectangular barns on the backstretch. The barns had cinder-block walls and clay tile roofs. Carl could smell saltwater in the air as he shook hands with Forrest for the first time. Both men stood outside the shed row of Forrest's barn, just a few yards from Big Zip's stall. It was nearly dawn now. The horse pushed against the chest-high royal blue webbing. A gold F was right in the center of the rubber divider. From where he stood, Carl could tell little about the horse, only that it was interested in something. Big Zip stood with head high, ears pricked. Forrest's tussled hair held some silver. He wore a beige-colored hunting coat. His teeth were capped. He had started out training quarter horses in Texas and New Mexico, winning everything in sight there before turning to thoroughbreds. His career had peaked between the mid-eighties and early nineties, a time when he'd won two Preaknesses and a handful of Breeders' Cup races. In 2003, Tom Westfeld had hired Forrest to be his private trainer at a salary of a quarter million dollars per year.

Forrest slipped both of his hands into the pockets of his hunting jacket. The jacket had leather lapels and a leather collar and it didn't seem right for the weather. It's warmer than that, Carl thought. Forrest turned his shoulders in the direction of Big Zip. "We'll get him out in a few minutes," he said. Forrest and the horse watched one another. While looking at the horse, Forrest said, "Just gallop him a mile and a quarter. Start in the chute at the top of the homestretch. You feeling strong? Need me to put draw reins on him?"

"I feel good," Carl said. He held the riding whip he'd brought in his left hand.

"Good. Have you ridden on synthetic before?"

"At Turfway, a couple of winters back."

Forrest nodded at this. "Turfway."

"I've heard each synthetic surface is a little different though."

"What Westfeld is interested in is if the horse feels any different to you than it did."

"I understand."

Forrest seemed to be squinting mildly at Carl. "Actually, I'd like to know that myself." He waited for Carl to speak. Forrest said, "This the fastest horse you've ever been on?"

Carl considered his response. "Yes," he said. "It probably is."

Forrest smiled in a conciliatory manner. "I envy your position somewhat." He stood on his toes then relaxed again. Carl was about to respond when Forrest turned to the shed row and said to one of the grooms, "Preparese ese caballo. El Zipper." When he turned to Carl again, he said, "You win, you make us all look like a bunch of dumbbells. You lose, it looks like we just paid too much money for this horse in the first place."

Carl said, "I doubt anyone would call you dumb." He did not mean this as flattery. Forrest probably understood as much.

"Excuse me," Forrest said, then stepped in the direction of Big Zip's stall.

Inside the stall, a groom tightened a leather girth around the horse's midsection, then placed his hands on either end of the saddle and tried to slide it. The horse did not protest. Carl held his hands behind his back and tapped the end of the whip against his left calf muscle. Sunrise arrived in an instantaneous way. The groom brought the horse from its stall. Perhaps Carl's heart should have skipped a beat at this. He thought of the time he had been walking to the track kitchen to meet Christine and the sunrise had arrived just like it had here. In a snap. Life could be so wonderful in some ways. The groom led the horse over to where Carl stood and stopped a few feet away. Carl hadn't moved. He had decided that these two mornings were of equal significance. Ten years from now—or twenty—if he had to choose one over the other, which would it be? Which did he really have more of a say in? An easy call. Christine was something he went after, Big Zip had always been what fate had dealt him. Henry Forrest stood at Carl's side again and he said, "Look all right to you?"

"Where's Tom Westfeld this morning?"

"Hey-ho," Forrest said. "He doesn't come out at this time of day. You'll see him on Saturday. He likes the races."

"Oh, all right."

"The horse look the same?"

Big Zip was well mannered. Carl hadn't seen this dimension of the horse back at Summit. Back there, the horse seemed to have been plucked directly from an open prairie. No respect, no care, no clue. In a race, the horse was a high-speed train, everything just sailed by. Carl brought up his left hand. He stepped forward one step and tapped at the horse's muzzle with his palm. He studied Big Zip's eyes. They were marbly, a bit vacant, tamed. He understood that Forrest and the groom were watching him. Carl thought, What do you want me to do? Break down and cry at the sight of this horse? He said, "He was a little more unruly-looking last fall." He was looking in the direction of the groom when he said this. Carl shrugged and said, "I don't speak much Spanish. Caballo is horse, I know that."

"Yes," the groom said.

"Give him a leg up there," Forrest's voice said.

Carl walked to the left side of the horse, lifted his left foot like a flamingo. He felt the groom's hand around his ankle, and Carl was hefted skyward. Sitting in the saddle had him feeling like a giant. A handful of other horses and exercise riders appeared around him. "Boys and girls, this is Carl," Forrest said. There were murmurs, hellos. Then the small herd aimed for a wide concrete path between the barns. Carl turned to his right, said to the closest rider, "How are you this morning?"

"Good." The rider was a middle-aged Asian woman. More than a decade ago, there had been a Japanese girl, Trinh Iyoto, in the jocks' colony at River Downs, and Carl said, "Have you ever ridden in Cincinnati?"

The woman cut her eyes in Carl's direction. "Sorry, un-uh," she said.

"There was a lady jockey there, they called her The Bandit," he said. "She wore a bandanna over her nose and mouth when she rode. Didn't want to get windburn."

The woman regarded him in an amused way.

"She kicked my ass more than a few times."

He heard one of the riders laugh softly at this. The woman looked in the direction of the laugh, then regarded Carl again. "I'm sure she did."

"All right, you all, get going," Forrest's voice said.

3.

Later that morning, Carl sat up in bed in his hotel room and absently flicked the remote from one channel to the next until he finally just switched off the set altogether. He pulled an armchair over to a window in his suite that faced the hotel's huge, egg-shaped swimming pool. It didn't seem warm enough to swim, though the lounges that rimmed the pool were occupied, mostly by pale-complected people. Carl had yanked off his boots and pulled on his white robe, but otherwise he wore his riding clothes. He propped his socked feet on the window sill, watched the people around the swimming pool and wondered if he could do anything to keep Christine. They weren't going to last forever. Carl and Christine had both understood as much, even after it was agreed that he would live with her. He'd had to accept the offer to fly out here and ride Big Zip in a race. Not to do it would be admitting he was afraid to leave Christine alone for fear of the inevitable: that she would reconcile with her ex-husband, the gambler. A call from California was a rare thing, and if Big Zip finished up the track on

Saturday, Carl would never get another. He had to try. He had to be exactly where he was right now, but it wouldn't matter whether Big Zip won on Saturday. If Carl won or lost, Christine would not change her mind. If he won, she might even feel less guilty about leaving him, though it would belittle her to conclude such a thing.

He pictured the moment from earlier that morning when, right after daybreak, the groom led Big Zip from the stall and brought the horse over to where Carl stood, the groom and Henry Forrest both interested in his reaction. They'd expected to see more than Carl tapping at the horse's muzzle with the palm of his hand. He'd tried to appear indifferent. He'd thought, Are you the one? Can you be the one who can change it all for me? He didn't like to think this way because it made it seem like what he already had was insufficient. Far from plenty. He had spent a long time convincing himself otherwise.

Big Zip looked slick that morning, and Carl liked the idea of being on the horse's back again. Big Zip galloped confidently over the artificial surface. They passed the open-air grandstand on their way down the stretch. The rows of seats seemed to cascade down from the center of the sky. It took them no time at all to get past that. The clubhouse was a quarter the size of the grandstand and was fronted with a grid of blue-tinted glass panes. The only sounds were the gentle noises of the galloping horses on the track. If Carl had known very little about his work, he might easily have believed Saturday's race would be nothing more than a cakewalk. If a person wanted to be fooled into thinking something, that was their business. But all you had to do was look around. Each of the horses here seemed to be in wonderful condition. They trained in glorious morning air. The Pacific Ocean was right across the highway. The waitresses in the clubhouse dining room were probably just slight variations of Courteney Cox. All of this could keep anyone going forever, until the end of time. Things were good out here. You just needed to modify yourself. Turn believer.

Now Carl watched as one young man did laps in the pool. The man wore goggles, a yellow skull cap, and a dark blue Speedo. He seemed to possess an infinite amount of stamina. Carl checked his Timex, had it set to Summit time. He reached for his cell and dialed Christine. It was three o'clock in the afternoon there, before she had to go to work. Her voicemail answered, the beep arrived. Carl said, "Hey, it's Carl here. Out in California. Everything's fine. Listen, I was just thinking about something. I was named on a horse in the nightcap today at Summit, he's a seven-year-old, name's Holdfast. The horse has been running good, but they replaced me with Bill Hoyer, I think. Bill's not strong and he won't be able to rate that horse at all. Christine, I'd get out a *Racing Form* and handicap the race. Throw that horse out of all your exotics. He'll be favored and it'll burn a lot of money. Christine? It just hit me. I don't why I didn't call you about it earlier...Well, like I said, everything's fine here. Talk to you later."

Carl slipped the phone back into the pocket of his robe. He closed up the robe, had the folds stuck between his legs when the cell rang. It took him a moment to find it. "Hello," he said.

"It's Tab."

"Tab," Carl said. "Right."

"What about I drive over there and pick you up? Bring you out here to watch some races? You can see how the track is playing."

"I want to do something like that," Carl said. "Tell you what, I am not quite ready to go yet. I'll get a taxi and get over there myself."

"Want to meet me in the clubhouse or something?"

"Let me just get there and watch the races myself. Let me see what I can see. That okay?"

"Yeah, sure. They just want me to touch base with you."

"Somebody think I'm going to go crazy out here?" Carl said. "Hookers, dope, more dope, more hookers?"

"Happens every minute of every day."

"Maybe next trip. I'll see you in the lobby tomorrow morning, okay?"

"Good enough, I guess."

Carl hung up, remained in his chair. He looked down to the people around the hotel swimming pool. Carl didn't want to go to Balboa Park or any other racetrack today. It would be unprofessional of him not to, though, so he would. At least he could do it when he was ready. In a while, he walked over to the nightstand, dialed the front desk. The operator said Carl would need to let the bellman know if he wanted a taxi but Carl said, "Do it for me, please. The taxi is to take me to Balboa Park. I'll be down there in about twenty minutes."

A green car with black letters reading "Coronado Cab" on the passenger door was waiting for him when Carl stepped through the sliding glass doors at the hotel entrance. The driver was a middle-aged black man with a bald head and when Carl leaned into the open passenger window, the driver said, "Taking you to the track?"

"Right," Carl said. He decided to sit in the front seat.

The driver didn't appear surprised by Carl's decision. He tapped a button on the meter and red digits appeared; Carl already owed the guy a buck twenty-five. “You’re a jockey,” the driver said.

“That’s right.”

“Riding anything good?” Immediately, they were bogged down in traffic.

“I flew out here from Cleveland to ride a horse on Saturday. His name is Big Zip.”

The taxi moved forward a few feet before stopping again. The driver sat sprawled out in his seat. He touched his hand to his mouth. “Big Zip. I think I know that name.”

“Are you a horseplayer?”

The taxi moved forward again. “I am not.”

“Maybe you read something about the horse in the newspaper.”

He said, “No, not really. I guess it’s just one of those terms or something.”

Carl said, “He felt good today. Not that I’d recommend betting it, though.”

The driver nodded. “Oh. All right.”

Carl didn’t mind talking. He had only been here a day and didn’t want to feel sick of California yet. He tried to think of something else he and the driver could chat about. When they arrived at the entrance to the clubhouse at Balboa, the meter read $10.75. They had ridden along without speaking. Carl held out a twenty-dollar bill and said, “Just give me a five for change.” A nice tip. Carl said, “I do appreciate it.” He hoped the driver understood.

Carl exited the taxi and strolled to the clubhouse entrance. More sliding glass doors opened for him and inside he had to buy a ticket. Carl felt astounded at the intensity of the air conditioning. The clubhouse carpeting was like something from an

Atlantic City hotel, a pattern of big triangles, bright green-and-yellow ones. There were vendor stands for programs and *Racing Forms* and Carl bought two programs, one for Balboa and one for Summit. When he asked about the simulcast parlor, the good-looking kid selling the *Forms* swung out his right arm and pointed. Carl walked in this direction and a minute later discovered the simulcast parlor, wedged into one corner at the far end of the clubhouse. Scattered about were a few tables for two. One wall featured three rows of flat-screen TV sets. A wall perpendicular to this one offered betting windows. Two of the windows were occupied by actual people; the remaining half dozen featured automated teller machines. The programs felt like tissue in Carl's right hand and the ink had already smeared under the tips of his fingers. He walked closer to the wall of TVs. His eyes went from one to the next until he found the TV that featured a live shot from Summit Park. Racing had already begun at Balboa for the afternoon and the races were going on just outside. But they could wait. The nightcap at Summit happened to be a few minutes away. The horses were on the track for the post parade. The horse Carl would have ridden, Holdfast, appeared on the screen. It wore an orange saddlecloth with a white number 7 and an impassive-looking Bill Hoyer sat atop its back. An info bar at the bottom of the screen had the odds at 6–5. The betting public didn't seem to care that Carl had been replaced. Holdfast was a small gelding with big nostrils and on the TV set, the afternoon light in Cleveland seemed to be a yellowish green. The camera focused on the horse that walked behind Holdfast, the number 8. Carl understood that he should be on that TV screen right now. His eyes would be focused down the homestretch of Summit Park. To his right would be the largely empty grandstand. He would get to ride in this race and then he would get in his car and he could clean up, change back into his civilian clothes, and drive back to the apartment he shared with Christine. It had taken him a long time to find a setup he could appreciate. One phone call from a wealthy, meddlesome man and all of this seemed far away again.

He needed to do something. He glanced over the smeary pages of the program for Summit and picked out the second, third, and fourth choices. He walked to a betting window, where he boxed those three horses in exactas and trifectas. He made a fifty-dollar win bet on the second choice in the race, New Normal, who was ridden by Ilya Kamanakov's apprentice rider, Rafael Barrero. Carl had these tickets in his shirt pocket as the horses loaded into the gate.

Holdfast, as Carl expected, broke quickly and stole away from the others. Hoyer's black boot took the shape of a checkmark as he sat back in the saddle with his feet shoved forward, trying to rein in Holdfast's speed. Holdfast opened up three, then four lengths on the field. When they entered the far turn, they accelerated even farther away. Holdfast could be rated for only so long. Hoyer knew that to keep fighting the horse would rob it of energy. It led by more than a half-dozen lengths as the field turned into the stretch, and this was where the hard running began for the others. Holdfast was tiring and Hoyer was tossing the reins and just brush-stroking with the whip. Only with a hundred yards left in the race did the others begin to gain—and when they did, they gained fast. But they were too late to change anything. Holdfast held on to win by a neck.

Carl didn't gamble much anymore but losing a bet felt too familiar to him just then. He reached into his shirt pocket and crushed together his tickets with his hand. On his way outside, he dropped them into a trash bin.

The clubhouse was separated from the grandstand by a spacious paddock, one that featured a walking ring in front of a line of saddling stalls lined in handsome, rich-colored wood. The walking ring, like the track, was an oval. The border was a path of white sand and in the center grew bright, putting-green grass. The saddling area adjacent to the walking ring consisted of a dozen rectangular stalls side by side. They were not under any type of cover. When it rained, Carl supposed the horses were simply saddled in the rain. It couldn't be a frequent occurrence, not out here. He looked over the walking ring and the saddling area and tried to imagine a rainstorm. The picture in his mind seemed so beautiful he had to blink his eyes twice.

Carl strolled along a footpath alongside the walking ring. He wanted to sit in the open-air grandstand and it took him a couple of minutes to walk all the way to the far end. He strolled under the stands, under the shadows there, and then he took a walk up a length of steps that were constructed in the shape of a square corkscrew. At the top of the steps was the first row of the grandstand's second tier. He wanted to be up high. The second tier of stands was sparsely occupied with horseplayers. The horses for the second race jogged along the backstretch. Carl found an empty section to sit in. He grinned in wonder; he couldn't be any farther from the finish line. He held the programs for Summit and Balboa and to start, he placed the Balboa program at his hip. He leafed through the Summit pages, even though the races there had concluded for the day. When he glanced up, the horses were near the starting gate on the backstretch. He tried to picture himself out there, aboard Big Zip. He wondered then when his very last ride would be. This was something he didn't think of often because in one way it was difficult to imagine and in another it was not. It would be the result of a horrible spill. He could never picture himself one day simply saying I've had enough of this. The spill: he would hear the sound of hoofbeats, then a snapped ankle and then the weight of a horse would crash down on him. He would feel the bridge of his nose caving in; this would be the last thing. It wasn't a stretch to imagine this; a good many jockeys ended this way.

He decided to check his cell phone to see if Christine had called to give him a little grief about the horse he'd told her to bet against. There were messages from a couple of trainers at Summit. Christine, he supposed, wasn't checking her calls on a regular basis just now because she was trying to put her marriage back together. Even though it was her shift, she might not be at the Seven Seas. After Carl had left for California, she might have asked for a couple of days off. She and Michael would have long talks about gambling. Christine would be the one doing the talking. She would lay out things for him. She would explain that things were going to go a different way this time. Michael would listen and then when it was his turn to speak, he would talk about love. Christine would say, That's fine, but this time we're going to use our heads. We're going to be shrewd and we are not going to panic. Michael's life would be less than it was, but he would have almost all of it back. Michael had told Carl this much. When Carl got back to Cleveland, he could talk to Christine, explain to her that the odds would not be in her and Michael's favor, bit it simply wouldn't matter. When it came to Michael, she couldn't be reasoned with. She was in for a difficult future.

When Carl returned to the apartment, Christine might want to keep the arrangement going. He already knew that he would agree to this. He would simply create a new rule: No more talk about Michael. He appreciated her honesty and he had heard enough about Michael. He needed to focus on his riding. Carl would do his best in the San Diego Handicap and when he flew home after this, his business was going to get a lift. Even though Bill Hoyer had just won a race that Carl was supposed to. Carl was at Balboa Park because a rich man was willing to pay him handsomely to ride a good horse that had been losing since it had left the Rust Belt. Bill Hoyer would never be able to say such a thing, not in a million years.

The horses in the second race at Balboa broke from the gate. There was the call of the race on the P.A. system. Carl watched the race with a dry mouth. The horses headed for the far turn. On Saturday, that would be him, the man who might get Big Zip winning again. Carl imagined having the lead as the field for the San Diego 'Cap made their way around the turn. He tried to imagine all that could change as the result of a single race.

4.

The fifth race of the afternoon was at a mile and a sixteenth, and for this race, the starting gate was set halfway down the homestretch. The horses walked for the gate and a cluster of people gathered along the outside rail to get a good look at the start. Carl thought one of the people gathered at the rail might be an exercise rider from Henry Forrest's barn, the one he'd asked about Cincinnati. She had long black hair; wore jeans, a loose, untucked, white blouse. Carl watched her as the horses broke from the gate. The field headed for the clubhouse turn and Carl stood and began to walk down the steps of the grandstand.

Carl kept his eyes on the race as he moved down the steps. The horses traveled up the backstretch and he stepped onto the asphalt apron, began to walk in the direction of the exercise rider. The field made their way around the far turn and began their run down the homestretch. He focused on this. The jock on the 3-horse found an opening between rivals approaching the furlong pole and in a blink the 3 had the lead. It wound up drawing away, winning by a half-dozen lengths. Carl stopped ten feet from where the exercise rider stood. She was with some other people, a couple of women and a man. Civilians. She was the shortest person in the group by half a foot. At some point she would turn, and then she would have to see him. Carl had spent the night before in a nice hotel room and driven himself crazy. He didn't want this to seem obvious.

She turned to speak to the man standing there and seemed to catch Carl from the corner of her eye. She turned her shoulders, rolled her wrist and pointed in his direction with the butt of her palm. "Hey," she said.

Carl moved a step closer. "I saw you standing there," he said. He tilted his head back. "I've been sitting in the stands, watching the races. Thought I'd shuffle down and say hello."

The three people around the exercise rider were focused on Carl. He moved forward, kept his hands in his pockets. "I'm riding in the San Diego Handicap on Saturday," he said, in their direction.

"What's your name again?" the exercise rider said.

He told them. Carl pointed at her, then returned his right hand to his pocket. "You're Mariko, right?" he said.

"That's right."

"You all have the winner of that race?" he said.

"We weren't betting," one of the women said.

"Her boyfriend was on the six," Mariko said.

"He's not my boyfriend," one of the women said.

Carl said, "Mind if I hang out with you guys for a little while?"

None of them spoke and he considered adding, *I don't know anyone here*. But that wasn't the way to handle this.

"We were going to watch a couple more races," Mariko said.

"Here," the man standing by her said. He put out his hand, leaned in Carl's direction. "I'm Foster. That's Allison. Dancy. And you know Mariko, obviously."

"Not obviously," Mariko's voice said.

Carl shook with him. "What do you do, Foster?"

"Oh," Foster said. "A little of this and that."

"He's done some modeling," one of the women said.

"When I was, like, seven," the man said. Foster stuck his hands in the pockets of his chinos. He shrugged for some reason.

"Can I buy you all a drink?" Carl said.

Foster shrugged again. "Absolutely."

The shadow of the grandstand almost reached to where the five of them stood. One of the women turned and watched the horses being unsaddled. She was finally nudged along by the other woman. Carl waited for the group to walk past him and then he began to follow. He stayed a step behind Mariko, though he did not walk directly behind her. There were concessions at ground level selling ice cream and tofu dogs. The five of them wound up standing at a cocktail bar just beyond a line of parimutuel windows. The bartender wore a green vest and a khaki-colored shirt. Carl asked for red wine. Mariko ordered Riesling. She didn't say much, though the members of her group were polite and appeared to be mildly intrigued by him. The other women had twenty-five-year-old figures, forty-year-old faces. He told the group of them about Summit Park. He mentioned the glassed-in grandstand, what the weather did to the surface of the track. Without the benefit of any type of transition, he mentioned he was staying at the Lemon Grove Hotel. Foster nodded at this. He said, "That place is fun."

Carl was careful not to look at Mariko when he said, "I'm going to be there later. If you all need a fifth or sixth wheel or something. Call me." He didn't want to say his room number. "My last name is A-r-v-o."

"Yeah. Yeah, we might do that," Foster said.

The bartender seemed to be waiting on them.

"Here," Carl said. He reached for a pocket, walked to the bar counter. He wondered if Mariko's friends were looking at him while he paid the bill. When Carl turned, he said, "Cheers." He raised his glass, then took a drink. He stayed at the bar counter.

Mariko waved at him with the hand that was not holding a drink. "Bye," she said.

5.

Tab picked Carl up early the next morning. Carl had Big Zip on the track for a workout around sunrise. Henry Forrest asked Carl to have Big Zip gallop for a mile then run hard for an eighth of a mile—a one-furlong drill, "just to see how fast you can get him to go." Carl wanted to know this himself. The one-mile gallop went smoothly and nearing the eighth pole Carl shrunk himself in the saddle, rattled the reins. Big Zip catapulted forward and when Carl brought the whip out to the horse's periphery it felt like the horse was going to vaporize, it moved so fast. He brought his hand back to better control the reins, saw he still had the whip. Past the finish line, the horse eased itself, galloped out with its head down as Carl stood up straight in the saddle. Back at the barn the trainer didn't say anything about the workout; anybody could see it had been an excellent one.

Tab walked Carl up to a brick, ranch-style house next to the track kitchen that housed offices for the chaplain, the head of the horsemen's union, and the track stewards. Carl and Tab strolled down a hallway to see about getting Carl a California jockey's license. Much of the work had already been done. A secretary handed Carl a folder with a printout listing the previous licenses he'd held, the suspensions he had served, the fines he had paid—nearly every jockey had a similar history. Carl felt Tab watching as he looked over the file.

Tab held over a ballpoint and said, "Want to change something?"

"Signing off on it." Carl signed and gave the pen back to Tab, then stood and walked the folder over to the secretary. "Good to go," he said.

"We just need to take a photo," she said. "We'll have the card delivered to the jockeys' room this afternoon. Pick it up then." She was nice-looking. Middle thirties, short brown hair, breasts like cantaloupes. "Just walk down that hallway."

Carl pointed over his shoulder with his thumb. "My assistant will take me." He hoped she could see that he was joking. Carl turned and said in Tab's direction, "I got this." Tab grinned about something.

The secretary said, "Through there. You'll see."

The photographer was already set up and seemed to be waiting for him. She pointed to an empty stool in front of a royal-blue curtain. She too was nice looking. Carl wondered if anyone ever got tired of all this. She said, "Smile, please."

Back at the hotel Carl donned the white robe and picked up the phone to call room service. He could order a huge entree, then just vomit it back into the nice clean toilet an hour later. Carl, at one time in his life, had been a smoker, and when he'd been a smoker he hadn't minded flipping a meal as much because there was the cigarette he could smoke afterward. He'd quit smoking because of the coughing and the sickness he felt after a coughing spell. Once he'd stopped smoking, the practice of flipping a big meal became more complicated. The taste of vomit made him feel worse than sick; it made him feel despair. He decided instead to accept that he was a jockey, that the job never stopped, and that he should be grateful for that.

Carl lifted up the phone from its cradle. He asked room service if they had swordfish on the lunch menu and when the voice on the other end said yes, Carl ordered a child's portion, broiled, with lemons on the side, a shaker of pepper, a bowl of grapes, and a pitcher of chilled tap water. He supposed the hotel received a lot of picky orders like this because the person on the other end offered no objection. Carl hung up, sat on the edge of the bed and ran his hands through his hair. He didn't want to think about anything else so he thought about how Big Zip felt going full tilt just a short time ago. If Carl rode horses like Big Zip on a frequent basis, the glorious speed it possessed would not feel so unearthly. He thought of something he'd once read in a book about the history of horse racing, that the great jockey Eddie Arcaro once rode a horse that ran so fast it scared him. Carl thought the horse was Citation or Whirlaway or Coaltown, and he tried to recall the photos of each of these horses in the book. Everything was in black and white—that's what Carl was able to recall.

Arcaro had come and gone as a jockey generations before Carl even arrived. Every story Carl had ever heard about Arcaro suggested he was a vicious bastard. He'd grown up poor and hungry in some godforsaken river town in Kentucky. He'd survived because he turned to riding when he was still a kid. He got out of his bullshit hometown, made a huge name for himself. He had been the most famous jockey in America, and after he retired he put on a yellow sports coat and did color commentary on races for ABC's *Wide World of Sports*. Arcaro's face had hard lines to it. When he talked about a race he didn't swear on camera, but he looked like he wanted to. He had been dead for more than a decade now and Carl was glad Arcaro had come along when he had because it would have made him sick to see the great jockey all shined up and sitting inside an ESPN studio. Carl would have liked to talk with Arcaro about the horse who'd run so fast it had scared him. Carl wanted to know if, just for a second, Arcaro had a taste of the afterlife on this holy-fast horse.

There came two taps on the door.

Carl was hungry, and he wanted to make everything about the meal last for as long as he possibly could. He carried the plate with the swordfish over to the bed and sat there and watched the activity at the pool. The fish had an amazing flavor; every bite seemed like a full meal. He'd ordered a child's portion, but he couldn't finish it. He set the plate by his hip and knew that if he sat there long enough he would grow hungry again.

6.

Carl decided to catch another taxi that afternoon and head back over to Balboa Park. The day before, he'd sat in the grandstand and watched the races unfold in front of him. How closely he had followed them was another subject. Some horses had won on or near the lead. Other races were won by late closers. Six furlongs—three quarters of a mile—was the distance of the race Carl would be riding in tomorrow. The race would be over in approximately one minute and ten seconds. He was going to ride a fast horse, and when the gates opened for the San Diego Handicap, Carl would send him to the lead, try to open up on the others. Big Zip might remember how easily they'd won races together last fall. Carl would ride the horse capably, but there was nothing he could do about how the horse would feel about him. Carl couldn't do anything about the weather, nor the condition of the track nor how it was playing. Henry Forrest knew this and Tab knew this. Overall, the idea of witnessing an afternoon card of races had seemed nothing but a needless test of his professionalism.

Nonetheless, Carl would watch a few races today. The races would make him feel more like a part of things. His main tasks this afternoon, however, would be to check in at the jockeys' quarters, pick up his license, and perhaps even introduce himself to a few of the other riders. Carl had checked the jockey standings at Balboa Park in the *Racing Form*. He had ridden against a thousand riders in his life. It seemed probable to him that one or two or even more of them would have wound up plying their trade on the elite Southern California circuit. Certainly a small number of the thousand or more had the talent to do so. Any one of them could have had such luck. When Carl looked over the list of names at Balboa, however, he supposed he hadn't ridden against any of these people. He had heard of practically all of the riders, though. Here were the names of jockeys who'd regularly had mounts in Triple Crown races. There were Breeders' Cup trophies on the mantles inside their homes. These people had BMWs and personal trainers. If he had seen the name of anyone he'd already ridden against, Carl wouldn't have felt as compelled to pay a visit to the jockeys' quarters a day before his race. On raceday he would have someone to look for, someone to shoot the breeze with for a few minutes. This was all he would need to help calm his nerves. But there were no familiar names. He needed to get some things over with today. Tomorrow, he was going to be a little jumpy; there probably was no way around that. The last thing he wanted to do was to show it.

Carl rode to the track in a taxi driven by a put-out-looking man. Carl rode in the front seat like he had the day before and once they had been going for a minute, he gave up the idea of starting a conversation. When the stands appeared in the distance, Carl said, "There will be an employees' entrance. Pull in there. There should be a sign that says Jocks' Room." The driver glanced at him. Carl said, "My name is Gustavo Avila. I won the Kentucky Derby in seventy-one."

The driver glanced to the highway, then back at Carl. "My name is Donny Osmond," he said. "I'll do anything for a check." They rode in silence until the taxi idled in front of the entrance to the jockeys' quarters. A blond-haired man sat on a metal fold-out chair near the glass doors of the entrance. The man was tall and bony-looking. "Here you go," the driver said.

Carl held over a twenty-dollar bill and waited for the change. He offered the driver a one-dollar tip. The driver hesitated before he accepted it. "That Derby was a long time ago," Carl said.

"You're the most," the driver said, as Carl pulled himself out.

The taxi eased away and the man from the metal chair stood. Carl said, "I'm riding in the stake tomorrow. Big Zip. The racing office licensed me, they were going to send the license over here..."

The security man nodded as soon as Carl had begun to speak. He held a walkie-talkie near his chin. "Carl Arvo is here," he said into it. "Tell Wes."

"He'll be waiting," the voice in the walkie-talkie said.

"Roger," the security man said.

"Send the jockey ahead, please."

The security man lowered the walkie-talkie. He stepped farther to the side and said, "Go ahead. Straight down the hallway are the men's lockers. Someone will be waiting for you."

"Great," Carl said. He felt as if he ought to shake the man's hand, but decided against it. He pulled open a glass door, walked down a hallway, spotted the door with a small window at the end of it, noticed a man's face in the window. When

Carl was just a few feet from the door, he thought the guy said, "Arvo." The man who opened the door had a wiry build and yellow-gray hair at his temples. His eyes were blue and a bit bugged-out. "It's Wesley Dade, Carl," he said. Carl noticed the man wore a uniform, light gray slacks and a matching button-down short-sleeved shirt with the word 'Wes' stenciled over the pocket. "I heard you was coming out here to ride." Wesley released Carl's right hand, then patted his left elbow.

Carl said, "Wesley Dade, rode at Mountaineer Park."

"That's right. I saw the overnight sheet, your name on there. I told Evelyn, the security guy out front. I said, 'Lemme know when he gets here. We go back.' I thought I might see you tomorrow...you got something else today?"

"We do go back, Wes. Long time."

The locker area looked large enough for a half-court basketball game. The lockers had no doors, were made of dark wood. Lockers lined the walls to his left and right; they held hectic-looking collections of helmets, whips, flak-jackets, shoes, pants, socks. Fold-out chairs faced the lockers, a few were occupied by male riders. They wore wife-beaters, white or black riding pants. The floor, a green-and-white checkerboard tile, held scuffs, heel marks. No one sat close to anyone else. One of the riders flossed his teeth. Above a row of lockers a flat-screen TV showed the in-house simulcast feed. On the screen, a neatly kept man with gray hair held a microphone. He stood next to the actress Bo Derek. She wore an Australian hat and they stood in the saddling ring, the grandstand beyond them. Bo Derek stood a head taller than the man. The man smiled throughout the interview.

"You work here, Wesley?" Carl said. He hoped he sounded impressed.

"Sure. You oughta see the lady jocks' quarters. They got a chandelier in there. A piano player."

"What?"

"No. How would I know?"

Carl shook his head.

"Say, what happened to that woman you were with at Mountaineer? She was something."

Wow, Carl thought. I don't know who you are referring to. He swallowed and said, "You should see the one I'm with now, Wesley. Late twenties." And kind, he thought.

"I married Jesse St. Pierre," Wesley said. "For a while. Remember her? She worked in the gift shop at Beulah Park."

Carl grinned, felt a puff of air escape his nostrils. Wesley did not expect him to remember. Probably not unless Carl had slept with Jesse St. Pierre, and maybe not even then. Overall, it seemed to be an incredible stroke of good fortune to find Wesley Dade here. "Listen," Carl said, "they sent my license over. Where can I pick—"

"Want to meet some of the guys, Carl?" Wesley tapped at Carl's stomach twice with the back of his hand. Carl stood with his hands on his hips. He shrugged because he thought Wesley would like this.

He led Carl down a length of lockers and then they went to the other side of the room and walked along the other. Wesley nodded to some of the riders, others he introduced. Some of them nodded in Carl's direction. None of them got to his feet and just a couple of them put out a hand for Carl to shake. Wesley was a valet. He shined boots for riders and helped keep the locker area neat. He kept the equipment clean and organized, best as anyone could. Part of his job was to make sure there were plenty of fresh towels available. All of the riders seemed to understand the situation. While he introduced Carl around, none of the riders asked Wesley to fetch them anything. Carl and Wesley wound up near the door with the square of glass at a rider's eye-level. Carl's insides were turning like blobs in a lava lamp. He couldn't recall the last time he'd felt so grateful to another rider. It wasn't because he had just met some famous jockeys. It was because he had gotten this part over with. He'd made an effort to be respectful and polite. Tomorrow, he didn't want to show up and appear to be in awe of the moment. He didn't want to feel grateful, like he owed anyone a thing.

Carl gave a quick sniff. "I do want to pick up my license, Wes."

"They assigned you a locker in another room," Wesley said. "I'm sure they had the license placed in there. I'll—"

"Let me."

"I got it, I got it," Wes said, patting at the air with both hands. He walked away from Carl in quick, short strides. He didn't limp or walk with a hitch. Wesley had done enough for Carl, but he wanted to keep it up. Which, in part, had to do with looking like he didn't mind any of this. He brought back a letter-sized manila envelope. Without asking Carl, Wesley opened the envelope and brought out a laminated card. He held the card up and turned it to catch the light at different angles, as if it were a prism or a jewel. Carl couldn't decide if he ought to reach for his pocket.

In a lowered voice, Carl said, "What are you drinking these days?"

Wesley's arm lowered, his expression fell.

Carl shook his head. He hadn't smelled liquor on Wesley. "I gotta get out of town right after the race tomorrow," he said. "I want to bring you something."

Wesley leaned closer. "Scotch," he said. He placed the card inside the envelope and held it to Carl's chest. "You can leave it in the bottom of your locker if you want."

"I'm happy I saw you," Carl said. "Feels like good luck."

"I'll see you tomorrow," Wesley said, beating Carl to it. "I oughta get back to work now."

"Yeah."

"All right."

Carl left the room, walked up the hallway. He nodded to the security man, who was now on a cell phone. Carl walked across the employees' parking lot toward the grandstand. He had just met Martin Infante, Sal Doringinac, Dominic Feathers. Infante and Feathers had mounts against him in the San Diego 'Cap. There were other riders there. There were eight horses running against Big Zip tomorrow. Carl could feel something now, a sense that he might be all right here. Not forever, but for one afternoon, maybe even a couple. He walked in the direction of the grandstand entrance, paid the three-dollar admission, then strolled to the program stand and bought one for the Balboa races, which were already going on.

7.

Carl didn't see Mariko at the races that afternoon, but she phoned his room that evening. He was in his white robe, sitting in the living-room area of his suite and looking over the room service menu. On the TV the sound was down as Barack and Michelle Obama walked across the White House lawn; they held hands and the wind stirred around them. Carl offered to meet Mariko downstairs for a drink. Instead, she asked for his room number. While he waited for her, Carl tried to decide about the robe, whether he ought to greet her while still in it. He didn't want to appear as if he had expectations. He tried to decide and there came a knock at the door and because he hadn't been able to decide, he wore the robe to the door. Mariko wore a light green dress with a slender black belt. She had on high heels and carried a purse. Her hair was cinched up in a bun at the back of her head. She looked tired. She said, "Hello, Mr. Timberlake, how are you?"

Carl said, "Do you want to go out? I can change."

"Are you going to let me in?"

He stepped to one side. Mariko dipped her head and walked by him. She took a few steps into the suite and then she stopped. She turned partway and said, "I could use a drink."

"There are airline bottles in the little fridge there," he said, nodding.

"Make me something, will you?" She walked across the suite, to the window that looked down to the swimming pool.

Carl went to the refrigerator, opened the door, and looked inside it for a time. "Do you have a beer?" he heard her voice say. He removed a sixteen-ounce can of Stella. He opened it and removed a clean glass from the shelf over the refrigerator. He carried the glass of beer over to her and she turned as he approached and accepted it.

She took a sip.

"What are you up to today?" he said. "You own a horse or something?"

"I've been visiting my son at SDSU," she said. She considered his expression, then said, "San Diego State."

"I figured it went something like that. You have a son, huh?"

"That a dealbreaker?" Mariko wore make-up today. She was pretty enough, but in a different way.

"I have a son and two daughters," Carl said. "Two ex-wives. That's how I roll."

Mariko brought the glass to her lips again. She took a drink, swallowed. "Actually, I'm not sure why I am here."

"Yeah, I get that sometimes." He wanted to enjoy this, whatever it was they were about to do. He was ready for company, but it seemed especially good to have the company of another rider. "You wanted to see how a real jockey has it," he said.

"Dom Feathers has a house that looks out over the Pacific Ocean," she said. "He wasn't even the leading jock here last meet. My friends and I go to parties there."

"Right."

She said, "Do you mind if I ask you a question? How can you spend so much of your life riding bad horses? Just for fun, my friends and I Googled you. We went to the Jockeys' Guild page. Aren't you just totally over that?" She took a drink and watched him. She was trying to anger him. She meant business. She was probably curious, as well.

Carl said, "Bad horses can win races."

Mariko looked at him in a kind way. She turned her shoulders, glanced to the window that looked out on the pool. "When I came up, I rode at Portland Meadows. Yakima. Hastings Park up in BC," she said. "I'm not superior. I don't want you to think that about me."

"You get hurt?"

Her eyes were on him again. "I just grew out of it. I had a chance to come to Balboa and exercise horses. No more race rides," she said with a shrug. "When I was young, it was this act of rebellion or something. My father, let's just say he didn't respond well at all to that. I ran away to the races, to the bad racetracks. Yakima, first. I rode the fairs, too. Santa Rosa, Stockton. Bull rings." She moved the glass close to his chest. "Very, very dangerous."

Carl couldn't decide if she wanted him to take the glass. He didn't reach for it right away, but then he did. He lifted the glass from her hand and said, "Good horses break down."

She blinked. "Sure they do. But that's the cosmos. That's the way it goes. But you're not asking for that kind of trouble when you're on a good horse."

"That all depends." He thought about kissing her right then. He couldn't tell if what she was giving him was a sign. If this were Cleveland, it would have been plenty. He said, "I'm risking something by coming out here." He had not made any type of move towards her but now Carl leaned closer. "Back in Cleveland, my girlfriend is probably getting together with her ex-husband right now." He decided to lean back some. He took a drink from the glass of beer. "You don't need to tell me about trouble, lady."

Mariko fixed her eyes on him. "Is that why you found me, because of your girlfriend?"

"I found you?" he said. "You were there. But, yeah, she is about to screw me over. Tell me why you're up here. Your son tell you you were a bad mother?" It wounded her, he could see that right away. He hadn't meant to hurt her, he just wanted to keep up with her. Her mouth was closed and her jaw muscles knotted at the corners. He was about to apologize.

She said, "My friends dared me to come up here to see you. They said, 'Pay that guy a visit. See if he's got any game.'"

"I don't have any game at all," he said. "I'll save you the trouble." It was uncomfortable now. It had been that way since she had stepped into the room, but now it was too much. He was riding in the San Diego Handicap tomorrow and flying home after the race. He said, "Let me treat you to dinner. I got this menu in here."

"I'm a good mother, asshole," she said. "My son has a motorcycle. I am trying to talk him into selling it. You don't have to wear a helmet in this state. That's a real concern of mine."

"So, this is your mother look?"

"Sometimes casual doesn't cut it. Once in a while he calls me by my first name. I don't like that. His father's a tall man. So is he."

"My son is a salesman," Carl said. "I hear he's good at it. Here." He held the glass of beer back to her. She shook her head. "Will you stay for dinner? It's on the house," he said. "Please."

She did not answer.

"I'll bring you the menu," he said.

Mariko ordered a lobster salad and—at Carl's urging—a bottle of champagne. She slipped off her heels. He sipped from a glass of champagne and she ate her salad. They watched pay-per-view, something with Ben Stiller. After it was over, she excused herself, closed the restroom door behind her, and when she stepped out again, she was nude. She was slender and muscular and her hair was loose.

"What happens next?" she said.

"Everything."

Carl stood and shed himself of the ridiculous robe. They turned off the TV and had sex on the couch. Mariko lay on the couch afterward and covered herself with Carl's robe. Eventually, she fell asleep. Carl decided to sleep as well, and he went to the bedroom.

In the middle of the night, he awakened. It was well past two and he wanted her to get into bed with him. Mariko was gone, however. The white robe was folded on the couch. Carl walked over to it and ran his hand across the fabric. He sat down next to the folded robe. After a time he said, "I wanted to tell you about Big Zip." He stayed quiet after this and tried to imagine where Mariko lived and what type of life she had. Something like his, but with better furniture. In Cleveland, he would have to work harder to get a woman like this. What would she say if one of her friends asked, What about that guy who came out here to ride Big Zip? He thought of how Mariko might answer. *I went up there to see him. Wants it all. Nothing unique.*

Carl returned to the bedroom and crawled back under the covers. He hadn't phoned Christine yesterday, though he had thought about doing so on any number of occasions. He'd felt the greatest urge to do this while he sat in the grandstand and watched the races. He wanted to tell her about the jockeys' quarters and some of the famous riders there, to tell her how he felt because this specifically had surprised him. He thought about how he wanted to describe it. He would say, I have not felt any age in particular for the past month or so, since I have been with you. He thought that she would like this, and on a couple of occasions he had taken his cell phone from his shirt pocket and stared at it. It was the middle of the afternoon at Balboa and she would be at work already—if in fact she had reported to work.

Carl had talked his way into Christine's apartment because she was vulnerable. She had been cleaned out by her former husband and she needed something else to happen in her life. She'd been ready for a few winners. Carl hadn't been living with her for long, five weeks all told. He didn't want to get her voicemail again. They hadn't talked one time since he had left for California, but he understood that she was telling him something. He lay awake in bed and thought about the rest of his own life. It seemed like a good enough time to do this. He was in a comfortable bed in a suite in a hotel that had a clear, clean swimming pool, just across the street from the ocean.

He was not going to be a valet. He would be a jockey until the end. He formed an image in his mind of a skeleton riding a horse in a morning workout. He pictured this happening at Summit Park. He tried to imagine how the wind felt as it whistled through his ribcage. He wondered if his thoughts now were simply a way of protecting himself when it came to the idea of losing Christine. Christine *wanted to understand* the races, this was the thing that was pretty heartbreaking about all of this. How would this trip have gone if she had been with him? She would like this hotel. She would have liked what was in the distance beyond the racetrack. She was a Midwestern woman. He would have liked showing her off to Wesley Dade. That might have been better than riding in a race he didn't figure to win. Christine might have seen another side of Carl if she had flown out here with him. He understood that was partially why she hadn't wanted to join him. That it would make their split more painful.

"Well, I'm here, goddamnit," he said. He spoke these words aloud, before he knew anything else. His heartbeat quickened and he sat up in bed. He reached for the switch at the base of the lamp on the nightstand. The light flickered on and it brought a bluish glow to the room. Carl set his hands on top of the covers, atop his thighs. He said, "I have a mount today. Eighth race, the feature. The horse I am riding is a good horse. Me getting to ride him in the first place was nothing but dumb luck...If I can get in the clear early, I think I can win." He drew in a breath and then exhaled. "I wouldn't gamble the plantation on this. But a little something, sure." It was a true assessment. He felt exhausted. He lifted his right hand and softly snapped his fingers. What would happen would happen, just like that. Or it wouldn't. He reached over, switched off the light. He slid under the covers, brought them up to his neck. Time, he thought, to get a little more rest.

8.

He didn't have to report to Henry Forrest's barn on the morning of the race. There would be no morning workout; Big Zip would only walk the shed row, and the horse would be riderless during this time. Carl watched TV, ordered coffee, paced about the room. By ten a.m. he was packed and ready to check out. It was still too early to ride over to the track. He lingered in his room until he could no longer stand being in there. He phoned down to the front desk and asked for a taxi, then walked over one more time to the window that looked down to the swimming pool. The race wasn't until four thirty in the afternoon. He stood in this place for a minute and then he departed the room for good. He rode the elevator downstairs, and after the doors opened at floor level, he carried his suitcase past the registration area and headed for a set of glass doors that led to the pool. He found an empty chaise lounge, set his case next to it and stretched out. He folded his hands atop his belt buckle and closed his eyes. He listened. A child laughed. A few young men talked amongst themselves. Carl had done enough to prepare for the race. He could enjoy the free time he had left. The young men went on about a woman; she had told each of them a series of lies. One of them said he would talk to her soon and then they all were quiet for a time. Carl remembered he had called a taxi, but he allowed himself another minute.

Finally, he snapped up from his lounge, grabbed at the handle of his case and headed back inside. Somehow, he felt scolded. He walked across the lobby, and through the glass doors of the entrance he could see the taxi parked along the front curb. He walked right out to the taxi, to the rolling-down passenger window. He stuck his head in, said, "Hang on. I still have to check out. You can start the meter if you want."

"Already have."

On the way to the racetrack, Carl asked the driver to find a liquor store. The driver pulled up to one called Bigfoot Booze, and Carl took his time inside the store. He wanted to buy Dewar's for Wesley Dade. When Carl returned to the backseat of the taxi, he carried a pair of one-liter bottles of scotch with him. He unzipped his suitcase and worked them into it. The driver's eyes were in the rear view. In that direction, Carl said, "All right, let's go."

Carl wondered if the driver was a gambler. If he was, he probably couldn't decide whether it was a good idea to bet against a drunk jockey or on one. The driver stopped at the entrance of the jocks' quarters at Balboa and Carl held a twenty-dollar bill between the front seats and didn't wait for change

Inside the big locker room, Carl didn't spot Wesley Dade right away. He walked down the middle of the room, the lockers on either side of him, and he understood that any number of the riders seated on the benches might have been looking his way. It didn't matter today whether he said hello to any of them. Yesterday, Wesley had introduced Carl to some of the fellows primarily because Wesley understood that, for a few minutes, he didn't have to be a valet. He was someone who had been out there riding, too. For any of the riders to ignore him would have been an act of professional cruelty. It would have been bad luck for them. Today it would be all about winning and Carl would have a leper-like status.

The visiting riders' room had once been a shower; it had tiled floors, a drain right in the middle. Against one wall stood a half-dozen metal lockers with an aluminum bench in front of them. One of the lockers had a piece of masking tape under the eye-level ventilation strips, and Carl's name was written on it.

Apparently he was the only out-of-town rider here today.

Carl thought it would be all right if he took a quick tour of the place. Any rider new to Balboa would do this. He discovered the jockeys' quarters had a sauna, a weight room, a rec room, a sleeping room, and a kitchen. He happened into the silks room, where all the different designs of racing jackets hung from portable aluminum rails. Each owner had his or her own design and colors, and the silks here were organized by color. One rail held silks with red bodies or variations of red. Another held various shades of blue. Carl stood just inside the threshold of this room. It seemed like a strange museum to his own career, though he supposed any rider who happened on this room might feel the same. He thought, Goddamn, I've lost a lot of races in my life.

In a way Carl wanted to see Wesley, and in a way he did not. Carl had spent some time earlier this morning lying awake in bed trying to think of old Mountaineer stories for Wesley. He couldn't come up with anything specific. He thought of Mountaineer Park, and when he pictured the track and the stands there a thick mist covered everything. Carl supposed he'd ridden at too many different tracks by now. Memories sprang at him, he usually didn't go looking for them. Carl couldn't picture Wesley from back then in a vivid way.

While Carl toured the jockeys' quarters, there were other valets about, each of them in a uniform like the one Wesley had worn the day before. Wesley had been glad to see Carl yesterday, but then Wesley had to go home last night to whatever home was now. A retired jockey's home. A valet's home. Carl returned to the locker-room area and when he opened the locker with the masking tape on it, he the saw silks—green and gold, on a hanger, clean and satin-like—that he would be wearing during the race. He opened his suitcase and set the two bottles of Dewar's at the bottom of the locker.

He changed clothes, pulled on his white riding pants and a white wife-beater, and in his bare feet he decided to make for the kitchen. There were a few tables in there and a man in an unbuttoned chef's jacket stood behind a counter and chopped at a red onion with a small, shiny knife. On the counter were plates of cold vegetables and Carl reached for a celery stick. He held it so the man in the jacket could see. The man nodded okay and Carl nibbled at it. Then he tucked it in his mouth like a stogie. Carl finished the celery in the weight room, then eased himself onto an exercise bike. The other two bikes in the room were occupied by riders wearing earbuds. Carl pedaled steadily and in a while he went to the kitchen and retrieved another stick of celery. He chomped on the stick as he left the kitchen and finished it as he opened the door to the sleeping room. The light inside was brownish and only strong enough to reveal the outline of the cots. Carl picked out one with a metal frame and firm springs. The springs barely moved when Carl sat on the cot and slid under the blanket. He lay there for half an hour. Near the end of this half hour, his heart began to quicken.

9.

He met Tom Westfeld for the first time a few minutes before the race in the saddling area. Carl wore Westfeld's green-and-gold silks, a green cap-cover over his helmet and a set of goggles strapped just above the bill of the cap. He held his whip in his right hand. On his left bicep he wore a leather patch marked with a 4. Henry Forrest stood close to Westfeld and said, "Here he is," as if Westfeld would not be able to tell.

"Good to see you, Carl." Westfeld leaned down as if Carl were a dwarf. "I'm Tom."

"Hi, Tom." Carl nodded to Forrest and his eyes went out to the walking ring, where Big Zip paraded with the other horses. Their coats were showroom, their muscles seemingly formed from liquid metal. Carl didn't feel like speaking. For a moment, he didn't feel like riding. There were clouds, but the sky brought a handsome blue-gray light to things.

"Are you having a good trip?" Westfeld said.

Carl turned to him. He had both of his hands behind his back now. "Yes."

Westfeld watched Carl for another moment. Then he looked to Forrest and smiled.

"Get going early," Forrest said, and to this Carl offered a single nod. The trainer's expression surprised him, though. There was a spark in Forrest's eyes. *Okay, we're full of shit and we know it. Now show everyone.*

Two stalls down from the Big Zip contingent, a man with a microphone interviewed the connections of the number-2 horse, a man and a woman who continually nodded their heads. This was the man Carl had seen on the in-house feed in the jocks' room yesterday. Another man carried a video camera on his shoulder, taping the whole thing.

Westfeld stood erect, but there was a looseness to his frame. He was slender and toothy and tan. He wore light-looking clothes and his hair was windblown. He might have just come from a tennis match or be heading out to play in one. The three men were quiet for a time and they each had turned to watch Big Zip walk in the saddling ring. "No matter how it turns out, I thank you for coming," Westfeld said. "We had to try something."

"I know." Carl spoke quietly, without turning, and was not certain either man heard him.

The man holding the microphone walked up to Westfeld and Carl. Henry Forrest had slipped away. "This is Tom Westfeld and his rider," the man said with a nod to the camera.

"Hello, Anthony," Westfeld said. The men shook hands. "This is Carl Arvo. We brought him in to ride today."

"Hello, Carl," the man with the microphone said.

"Hello," Carl said.

"How are you going to ride your horse today?"

Carl rubbed his hand across his mouth. "He's going to ride Big Zip like he's the best horse in the race," Westfeld said.

"That's why we brought him out here." He glanced down at Carl and gave him another grin and a pat on the back.

Carl began to speak.

"Thanks," said the man with the microphone. "Well, it's about time for the post parade. So, let's toss it back upstairs to Donna and Roy." He watched the camera, waited for the man to lower it. The man held the microphone at his hip and turned his shoulders in Westfeld's direction. "Good luck, fellas."

Finally, the paddock judge called, "Riders, go to your horses!"

Relief washed over Carl as he finally sat atop Big Zip. The whole trip out west felt important to him again.

The horses, their riders now on their backs, paraded one last time around the walking ring. Out on the track waiting for them was a cluster of outriders seated atop their horses. Tab sat on a sweet-potato-colored quarter horse with a thick blond mane. When Carl guided Big Zip onto the track, Tab moved forward on his horse and reached for Big Zip's bridle. They joined the post parade and the horses walked in order of post position in front of the stands. Carl didn't look to the stands one time; he didn't care about that. Tab said, "The rail has been playing dead all day. Javarez, on the 3-horse inside you, might be pushing hard to get out of there early, so beware. Hey, how you doin' over there?"

"I'm gonna keep Big Zip a few paths out all the way around," Carl said. "He liked it that way last fall anyway."

"Perfect. Look, when we get under the finish line, I'll cut you loose."

"Thank you."

Once they were free from Tab, Big Zip went into an easy gallop. Carl crouched in the saddle, as if he were about to spring into action himself. He let the horse travel this way around the clubhouse turn. He tightened up on the reins after they went another furlong down the backstretch. The horse felt light under him, and Carl wished he could live the rest of his life just like this. He didn't need to know how it all would turn out. The horses were headed in a line for the starting gate.

Tab rode alongside Carl again. "Kick ass, man," he said. "I guess we'd love to see it."

"You'll look smart either way," Carl said.

"Huh."

Carl and Big Zip left Tab behind again. The horses for the race moved into the gate one by one. Javarez was in the stall next to him and he barked something in Carl's direction. Carl wanted to grin but he knew it was best not to react at all. He tugged the goggles down over his eyes. He was on a speed horse on a dry racetrack that with the sun baking smelled a bit like burning rubber. A few seconds into the race, Carl felt, his nerves would not be an issue—he was confident of that.

The starting bell rang; the field of horses sailed forward like a line of sprung arrows. Carl tried to ride. His balance seemed precarious, as if he were in the cockpit of a nosediving airplane. He closed his eyes and let Big Zip vault him forward. It was not a riding strategy. He heard a rider behind him yell out and Carl opened his eyes to find he was pinned by foes on either side of him. Tab was right, Javarez on the 3 was shouting and tossing his reins and hanging everything on getting to the front. Carl yanked on the reins. It would amounted to suicide to match strides early with any horse going all out like that, but Big Zip wanted to sprint, so Carl went with his horse and kept himself low, tried to make the lead. The horse to his outside fell back by half a length, but no farther than that.

The horses neared the turn and Javarez on the 3 took back, vanished like he'd found a trap door. He'd suckered them into a hot pace. Carl grabbed the moment, loosened the reins and they began to pull away. It was too early in the race, but Big Zip burned to be in charge. They hit the turn three lengths in front. Big Zip's ears were pricked and Carl allowed his eyes to find the stands in the distance. Easy, he thought—we're a part of this. Midway on the turn, he felt Big Zip slow just a tick, and he said "Easy" out loud. He loosened his hold, shook his wrists, let the horse feel all the give in the reins. Big Zip turned into the homestretch with a lead, but Carl could feel a wave of runners gathering in back of him. Big Zip was wilting, but he was trying, and Carl didn't want to ask the horse to switch leads until a furlong out. He could hear the race caller's voice, thought he could detect astonishment in it, but he couldn't make out anything else. Carl and Big Zip had an empty stretch and a huge sky before them. Carl stroked his arms forward and back on the horse's neck, he moved them with the stride of the horse.

Moments into the stretch a rival horse and rider appeared alongside Carl. They arrived so suddenly that Carl spooked. His weight shifted and Big Zip ducked in one path. The other rider had his hands in his horse's mane, his whip stuck straight up from his hands like an antenna. More horses were coming—that's how this jock was riding. This was the race, Big Zip couldn't let this horse pass them and Carl brought out his whip. He wanted to show it first, save the one stroke for a few strides from the line. He showed Big Zip the stick and the horse lunged forward, gave a grunt. Carl meant to tuck the whip away, just ride like crazy for another hundred yards. Then he saw the whip was gone. He was not holding it any longer.

"Yah!" he let out, bumped his boots on the sides of the horse. Big Zip veered out one lane, then another, and they brushed the rival at their side. The rider let out a "Yo! Yo!" and Carl grabbed the reins. The other horse and its rider jolted sideways and then that rider banged his boots to his horse's sides and they took off, opened up a quick lead on Big Zip. Other horses were gaining, arriving to Carl's right, and the race was over now. Big Zip flamed out, his racing heart had disintegrated. Carl couldn't keep riding. It felt as if he had swallowed an apple whole and he couldn't catch his breath. Carl felt as if he might collapse, might be the first jockey ever to die while still on the back of a running horse. The world had gone silent and he was passing from it; he couldn't tell anything else. All he felt was panic. He closed his eyes again.

The rhythm of the horse's stride brought him back. Carl opened his eyes, saw his hands moving atop the horse's mane as he rode the horse to the finish. He couldn't hear anything, but he had caught his air and told himself to breathe slowly. He pulled away the goggles. All the horses had passed them, each and every one of them—even the runner that fucker Javarez was on. It was never easy to ride out the final yards when you were in this spot and Carl had learned a long time ago there was only one way to do it and that was professionally. You kept your horse together and you kept it running. The public saw pulled up horses as horses in distress. Riders who didn't give them their money's worth. It seemed to take a long time to get to the finish line and when they did, Carl stood in the saddle and tried to feel nonchalant. He hadn't had to get involved in a wild speed duel early, but this was how Big Zip had run. The horse had done its best. It was not about confidence.

Carl thought what he would say to Henry Forrest. We were confident. It felt wonderful. And we still finished last. The whole thing had been a grotesque experiment, Carl Arvo at Balboa Park.

In the gallop out, he caught up with the others, and one rider yelled after him in Spanish. He kept yelling and Carl turned to say something, found himself wanting to know more of that language. He faced ahead again, eased Big Zip down to a walk. Everything had been made clear from the outset. He was their final hope with Big Zip. The horse was all right under him, walking soundly, but he was not good enough for California. "Man, you're beautiful," Carl said aloud, his voice thick. He didn't care that no one else heard him.

In front of the stands again, Carl dismounted, pulled away the saddle and carried it over to the weigh-out stand. The groom held Big Zip by a leather shank and then they began the walk up the homestretch. Everything had gone silent. Carl did the weigh-out, then held forward the saddle for the valet, a tall man with a thick mustache and curly, cotton-white hair. Henry Forrest stood out on the track by himself, and Carl knew he had to walk over there. He tugged at the Velcro band with the number 4 as he did. Forrest stood with his hands on his hips. Carl set his goggles above the brim of the cap cover. "I didn't save anything," he said, as he arrived in front of the trainer.

"Dropped your whip," Forrest said.

Carl felt the urge to apologize, but he knew better. That would be the worst. "He felt great under me," he said.

"There wasn't anything you could do," Forrest said. He said this after watching Carl for a moment. Carl hoped he didn't look like he needed someone to say such a thing. He swallowed and Forrest said, "Doesn't belong out here. That has been obvious for a while now."

It was not the worst thing he could have said.

Carl murmured, "Give me another chance, please."

"What?" Forrest said.

"I guess so," Carl said instead.

10.

When Carl stepped into the visiting jockeys' locker area, Wesley Dade sat on the bench. Carl had already unbuttoned the green-and-gold colors of Tom Westfeld, but they were evidence he'd ridden at Balboa and he wasn't in a hurry to shed them. Carl stopped a few feet away from Wesley, who turned and said, "I brought you tomorrow's edition of the Form. Midwest edition. It's got the races at Summit in there. You're named to ride in six of 'em. Booming business." Wesley motioned to Carl. "I'll take those," he said. Carl pulled away the colors. Wesley held out the folded *Form* with his left hand and accepted the silks from Carl with his right. He remained seated.

"Get the scotch?" Carl said, in a tired way.

"Thank you," Wesley said. "I tried to lay low this afternoon. I knew I might have caught you off guard yesterday."

"I was glad to see you."

"We don't get many jockeys from Ohio here. I saw your name in the entries and I couldn't believe it. I told these boys, I said, 'This guy can ride a little.'"

"I can, huh?" Carl felt like sitting down on the bench with Wesley. He remained on his feet. "I left some winners today back at Summit."

"They'll be there," Wesley said. He twisted himself a bit more in Carl's direction. "Javarez cost you. I knew that he would try something like that. He's nothing but a quarter-horse rider. I felt like warning him. I wanted to say to him, 'Look, the Carl Arvo I know gets his horses away from the gate quick.'" The skin on Wesley's neck was in barber-pole rings. He watched Carl's expression. In half a voice, Wesley said, "He thought he could outride you. You taught him that, anyway."

"I was nervous," Carl said, his voice quiet.

"You?" Wesley said like they knew one another better than they actually did. But this was not what he meant. He was being kind. Wesley lifted himself from the bench then. He faced Carl and put out his hand to shake.

Carl shook hands with Wesley. "Absolutely."

The nervousness stayed with him. It was there on the taxi ride to the airport, and while he waited at gate D3 for his flight back to Cleveland. Anyone would be uneasy, he thought. His future felt like a virus spreading inside him. It was the realization that the plan he'd made for his own life had been ill-advised. He was uncertain that he would be able to hide how he felt about it.

He flew first class going back. This, of course, had already been arranged. He tried to enjoy something. He drank two glasses of Cabernet. After the first glass, he understood that the wine would not help. Carl wondered if he was nervous mainly because Big Zip was gone for good. Ever since Carl had ridden the horse the first time, he'd imagined he was the sole reason it could run as fast as it did. If he'd ridden more good horses, he would have known better. A good horse made a passenger out of you. The bad ones, in the end, they made you crawl. They killed you. But maybe you felt desperate either way. Maybe good horses just put off the inevitable. Carl had held on to the idea that he was the magic man for this one runner. There was nothing wrong with him wanting such a thing, though all of the years he had spent as a rider told him better.

He tried for a time to fall asleep on the flight to Cleveland, but he knew he would see Christine in a matter of hours and the idea of this unsettled him. He had only been gone for a few days, but he knew better than to act like everything was the same between them. He had left on good terms with her, and they hadn't spoken to one another since. Carl hadn't wanted to burden Christine, but he needed to tell her he loved her. If it wasn't love, he didn't know the word for it.

Just the same, she wouldn't want to hear this. Carl gave the matter considerable thought. She hadn't allowed him to move in with her because of how either of them felt about one another. What was the more important thing, to tell her he loved her or to simply figure out a way to keep living with her? The cabin had darkened after the dinner-and-drink service ended and at one point Carl looked up at the shadowy figure of a female flight attendant standing over her him, asking if he would like a blanket.

"Thank you," Carl said and she unfolded it, draped it over him. Carl thought of the sound of his grandmother's voice when she'd checked on him at bedtime. She'd always said a prayer but he didn't think of that. The sound of her voice was what he thought of.

Under the blanket now, he felt more at peace. He was thankful that he was a grown man. He was thankful that only a short portion of his life had to be spent as a powerless child.

11.

He arrived in Cleveland near four a.m. Ohio time. Carl wished he hadn't canceled his morning workout schedule at Summit because he felt like getting on horses now, as many as could be lined up for him. He imagined driving to the track, yanking some rumpled clothes from his suitcase, and then going from barn to barn to see who needed a rider that morning. Too many people knew that he'd left for California and the San Diego Handicap. The result of the race was not yet twelve hours old. He shouldn't show up on the backstretch at Summit seeking work this morning. He didn't want it to seem like things really had gone so badly for him out there.

He drove for the apartment on this cold, black morning. It was late April. Christine might be there right now, sleeping alone in their bed. This was the best-case scenario, and he felt the rhythm of his heartbeat change at the thought of it. While Carl had been away, Michael could have easily said or done something mindless or unforgivable. Carl arrived at the Singing Bridge Apartments and parked in the slot assigned to their unit; Christine's car was not there. He opened the door to the apartment and it felt different than four days ago. He opened the bedroom door and didn't see her shape under the covers. Quickly, he flipped the light switch on and off. He turned it on and left it on. A minute later he turned it off. He walked out to the living room, where he had left his suitcase on wheels.

Carl needed to leave for the track just before noon, and that was when the front door to the apartment opened and in stepped Christine. She wore jeans, a sweatshirt, and a cloth jacket—white with brown patches on the elbows. Her hair was loose. Carl had not seen the jacket before and she didn't appear surprised to see him there. He sat on the loveseat. An open copy of *Metropolis* rested on his lap. He was glad to see her, but he was also fed up. She had never looked quite this beautiful. He held up the magazine with two hands and said, "Sustainably smart designs."

She said, "Why, there you are."

Carl lowered the magazine. "I gotta get to the track, Christine."

"I know." She walked to the kitchen and carried over a clear plastic chair.

He said, "The cat's gone. You could've told me that. You could've been up front about that. I wouldn't have gone to pieces."

"You were getting ready for California," she said. "Like the biggest race of your life."

"It wasn't…" Carl said. "You see—"

"I need to talk to you." She sat forward and clasped her hands together. Her eyes were dry and her expression had a blankness to it. She wore no make-up. Her freckles were so lovely. Christine said, "I am going to say what I am going to say and then I want to leave because neither of us is likely to be very happy. I simply don't think it's reasonable..."

"Tell me."

"Please don't get impatient with me. I just need you to listen and to think about what I'm offering. Carl, I'm moving out. I've already taken some things over to Michael's, and this week I'm going to move over everything else I need. I want you to keep this apartment. Here." She held out a folded piece of paper. "I started a bank account for you. Take it. There's almost five thousand in there. I cashed in the first-class ticket, deposited it. Take it before..." He did, and she sat back. "I still have five months left on the lease, and I will pay half the rent until the lease is up. You've made me money, and I have no problem at all doing this. We okay so far? Michael and I have been talking and we have a proposition for you." She decided to cross her legs at this point. "Tell me about your trip."

Carl lifted his hands then dropped them atop the magazine. "I won't be riding Big Zip again, Christine." He closed the magazine and placed it on the cushion next to him. "I closed my eyes during the race. Twice, actually. Dropped my whip at the eighth pole."

"You did what?"

"Surprise, surprise."

She swallowed at this and he felt like doing the same. He had planned to take the closing-of-his-eyes moments to the grave.

Christine said, "I thought you rode him fine. We watched the race at the simulcast parlor. I saw you being interviewed before the race, but it was too loud and I couldn't hear what you said. I was really pulling for you. You don't know how much."

"If I had won the frigging race, would it have changed any of this?"

"Of course not."

"Do you have something else you would like to tell me, darling?"

"Do you think you might want to stay here?"

"Christine, I have no idea. I have to leave for the track in about fifteen seconds."

She leaned forward again, reached one hand in his direction. She didn't touch him. "I know your schedule," she said.

"Jesus Christ, how bad is this?"

"Michael," she said. "We." She was leaning forward and now she held her hands together. "Wanted to ask you about a business proposition." She dropped her head and when she looked at Carl again, she said, "I can't go through with this."

"This is your apartment," he said. "You can't leave."

She decided to sit back in the chair.

"Why did you take the cat away before I left?"

"He was getting used to you. Bo traveled here with me and Michael. We got him from a shelter in Detroit. He was named something like Luke or Duke. But then we read about Obama's dog. We like the president's dog. This is our cat, Michael's and mine. Having you here…I don't know. It made me happy in a way."

"I never really had a chance with you. I knew that," Carl said. "Why did I keep trying?"

Christine said, "You fucking guys." She had her arms crossed.

"Stay with me, Christine."

"I am moving in with Michael. Didn't I just tell you that?" She brought her hand up and laid it flat on her chest, just under the base of her throat. "I married him. I was in love with him the first time I laid eyes on him. This is not what I am here to talk to you about."

"I've seen a million guys like him. They never change."

"You should talk."

He let that one go.

"It doesn't matter," she said. "I have changed. I have changed just enough. I learned something from you, Carl. Maybe it was something I knew all along. But you showed me what matters." She spoke carefully. "The most irresistible person in the room is the one who has the better idea on how the race is going to turn out. When Michael and I were first together, it was him. Now it's me. It just might be me. I know it and he knows it. I have the bank book to prove it. I want to participate in all of this, goddamnit. Carl, I want you to listen to me. Michael has an idea, and I told him that it might offend you. He thought we all might be partners. We would pay all of your rent and we would cut you in on a third of the profits. The deal would be that I would appear here every race day and have coffee with you. You would talk and I would listen just like before."

Carl didn't speak right away. In a minute, a calm arrived over the surface of him. "I thought you said you had a handle on things."

She said, "I'm trying to hold the good pieces of my life in place."

He pointed an index finger at her, but he didn't say anything. He set his hands in his lap again. "You're doomed."

She said, "No, I'm not. I would never think like that, not in a million years. Neither would…" A moment later, she got to her feet. She walked for the door and when she closed it, she did it in a quiet way, which hurt him as much as anything.

Carl left the apartment a few minutes later. He drove for the racetrack under a sky of gray and white swirls. He laughed at himself. Doomed. He wasn't trying to be cruel to her. This was the word that he had spoken, however. It could apply to so many things, so many levels of this life. It was a most accurate and most useless word in this manner. Still, Carl wished he hadn't said it—at least not to someone like Christine, who deserved better.

He understood that he was about to have a bad afternoon.

Before each race he rode in, he shook hands with the trainer, who would say something like, "I see you're back," or "Well, look who made it home." No one mentioned the race in California specifically. It was a difficult thing to say something positive about. Carl appreciated the politeness. He lost on all six mounts he had. After he dismounted and unsaddled, none of the trainers he had ridden for made an unfortunate remark about Big Zip or Balboa Park. On more than one occasion, Carl said to a trainer, "He just didn't have it today." This was fairly close to a criticism of the job the trainer had done getting the horse ready for the race, but none of the trainers he said this to showed any signs of irritation about Carl saying such a thing. He drove to Singing Bridge Apartments that night and sat at the kitchen table; he ate his tuna fast, directly from the tin. He wondered what other horsemen thought of him now. He imagined that they might believe his ride on Big Zip at Balboa Park was a heartbreaking experience for him. Horse of a lifetime, one more chance to sit on its back, and so forth. Carl had gone out to California to ride, but there hadn't been a lot of choice in that. The result of the race suggested he was simply a certain kind of man who needed to be in a certain kind of place. What he could do was always how he ought to be measured. He understood it was time to get an agent. He needed to change the focus from the result of the San Diego Handicap to the fact he had been asked to ride in it.

He knew that he would never be able to do this on his own.

He sat on the loveseat in the living-room area and opened his cell phone. He paged through the names on his contact list until he found Ilya Kamanakov and he pressed the green button to dial. The phone rang three times on the other end. Ilya said, "Cahl. Cahlavo."

"Ilya," Carl said. "I have been meaning to call you for some time now. Take you up on that offer."

"Hah, hah. Funny. That's funny. I am on death row. Remind me not to hire you for my lawyer."

"No, I wouldn't want me, either," he said. "Listen here, I'm just back from riding at Balboa and I am ready to start making some money. I think we can do it. It's not even close to summer..."

"Can't do it," Ilya said. "Cahl." He did not say anything else. Carl wondered if Ilya just liked the sound of the word.

"I know, you've already got Milord and that kid Barrero. Get rid of Milord. He's a stiff. I hear his arteries harden a little more every time I blow past him in the stretch."

"He's in the top ten of the standings."

"Bottom of the top ten," Carl said. "Come on now, let's win some races. Ilya, the only reason the guy is in top ten at all is because you represent him."

"Gary Shells is looking for a rider," Ilya said. "Man with a mustache. You know who I am speaking about?"

"Gary Shales? Yeah, I know who he is. He isn't as good as you."

"No, he is not. But he is looking for someone. I'm married right now, see? I leave Guillermo, I am a lowlife. I get a rep I don't need. Guillermo says he wants to go to Tampa for the winter. He wants warm weather. All that sunlight, it is too much for me. Call me after the meet in September. I want to stay up here."

Carl said, "You got a number for Shales?"

"No, I don't."

"If you see him…"

"I will." Ilya didn't hang up then. Carl supposed Ilya was waiting for him to do this first. He was a good agent. On his way up for sure.

"You watch the race?" Carl said.

"California? I did. How much you get? You mind me asking?"

"Five grand. You could've gotten me twice that, right?"

"Sounds like a lot to me," Ilya said.

"Sounded like a lot to me too."

12.

Two days later, Carl went to the track kitchen after morning workouts for a meeting with Gary Shales. The kitchen tables were crowded but Gary had secured a couple of seats at the end of one. The seat across from Gary was empty. He wore a straw hat with a green band around the crown. He was a tall, wiry man with a stooped posture, his age somewhere between thirty and sixty. He had a thick mustache and just his lower teeth were visible as he spoke. Gary was from out on the Great Plains and had ridden bulls and bucking horses until a quarter horse had fallen on him in a rodeo in New Mexico. He walked with a black cane, one that some hard-hearted people said he did not need. Carl approached the table and saw the cane leaned against an edge of it, near Gary's left elbow. Gary didn't stand and he and Carl didn't shake hands. Carl took the open seat across from Gary and they nodded to one another. Gary had a couple of unopened bottles of water in front of him and he picked one up and held it over. "Didn't know if you'd be thirsty."

Carl accepted the bottle, which felt cool and slick in his hand. He unscrewed the cap and took a long drink. He set the bottle on the table after this and glanced around the room. The cafeteria line was long, out the back door. Conversation seemed steady, like someone had left water running. Gary had chosen the time and place for the meeting, and he wanted people to see he and Carl might be going into business together.

Carl lifted the water bottle in front of him, considered the label, and then he set the bottle down again. "Whose book you have last?"

"Lori Wydick," Gary said. "Until last December. She promised her mother she'd quit the game. So she quit."

"Where is she riding now?"

"Sportsman's Park."

Carl said, "I haven't seen my mother for a long time now."

"Neither have I."

Carl felt a smile arrive at one corner of his mouth. "I usually do my own bookkeeping and make my own appointments. Monitor my own business. I feel like letting someone else do this for a while. Last Saturday, I rode out at Balboa Park. You see that?"

Gary Shales nodded his head one time.

"I stayed in a hotel suite that was bigger than the last two apartments I've lived in. When I got back here my girlfriend told me she had moved back in with her ex-husband."

Gary twisted the cap on his water bottle back and forth. "What can you do?"

"Remind people I was good enough to be asked to ride at Balboa. After that, just tell me where to go and what time to be there. I'll be at the top of my game in no time at all."

"All right."

"You ever hear anything about me, Gary? That I am unprofessional in any way? Something maybe a while ago? Be straight."

"A bit of a pain in the ass. Back in the day. Your rep now is you try. You're not afraid."

"I didn't know anything back then."

"Nobody does."

"What about talent?"

"What about it?"

Carl tapped his knuckles on the table top in a light way. He did this twice. "You got a family, Gary?"

"No."

Carl drew in a breath, then he sat back and reached into the pocket of the down vest he wore. He held out a set of folded papers. "We don't need a contract, do we? Not unless you want one. These are my schedules for the next two days. Includes morning workouts and afternoon races. I've already given a commitment to these people. You want to add to the lists, fine. From here on, you make the lists. I like to work, Gary. Okay?"

"Okay."

"Thanks for the water," Carl said. "Let's talk tomorrow night. Call between seven and eight."

Carl liked how the meeting had gone and when Gary called him the following evening, Carl was ready to talk. Gary, however, did not say much. This was his reputation, but Carl knew that sometimes this kind of person would talk a blue streak in front of certain people. Gary did not. On the phone, Gary spoke in three- or four-word sentences. He said things like, "Bourke's got a call. Fourth race, Friday. Looks fast."

"Good," Carl said. "Right."

"Willingham's filly for Sunday."

"Yes?"

"Told him we'd pass."

"Why?"

"Crazy."

"Don't worry about that, Gary."

"She sees dead people," he said.

Carl laughed. "Put me on her. What else?"

The entire call went this way. In a way, Carl liked it. Things seemed simple again.

At the end of it, Gary said, "Anything else?"

"Sounds good."

"Talk tomorrow."

Overall, Carl believed that the spring and summer were not lost—not yet. Gary was going to be a good agent, and if Carl could start winning races again, they might make for an excellent team. Gary knew horses and he was organized. Carl failed to win a race on Friday and Saturday, but these were the mounts he had lined up on his own. His touch wasn't there. His confidence was absent. Christine had moved out. Everything had turned to nothing. This had happened to him before. It simply got harder to deal with. He never wanted to act like any of this wasn't the truth. That would make riding and winning even more difficult.

Christine had apparently been showing up at the apartment during the afternoon races at Summit Park, collecting more of her things. Clothes, books, shoes. She could have finished the job faster and it meant something that she hadn't. Perhaps she had doubts about Michael. Who wouldn't? The guy was a floating crap game. If he wasn't risking something, he wasn't breathing, etc. There was going to be a ton of losing with a man like that. When Christine was with Carl, she could gamble, but it didn't have to be a personal statement. She actually could make a little money for herself, just enough to keep her interested in all of this. With Carl, she had a bit of a good thing going. So she moved out of the apartment slowly. It also could have been an apartment she liked. This was the place she had to herself after she kicked Michael out. She seemed, at least to Carl, to do fairly well on her own.

Carl went winless on Saturday afternoon at Summit Park and when he returned to the apartment late that afternoon, he found Michael sitting on the loveseat. Michael hadn't turned on any lights and appeared to be looking at the door after Carl closed it. Carl set his gym bag on the floor. Michael said, "She's not here, man."

Carl fought off a wave of uncertainty. He walked over to where Michael sat and grabbed the collar of Michael's dark, long-sleeve rugby shirt. Carl's fist clutched the fabric not an inch from Michael's jawline. Carl popped Michael's jaw with his fist before letting go.

"I don't care about anything, either," Carl said. "Just so you know." He stepped back, then turned and walked for the kitchen.

"Right. Whatever," Michael said after him.

Carl yanked open the door of the refrigerator and lifted out a partially full bottle of white wine. He stepped out to the kitchen table, he and Michael watching one another.

Michael brushed at his collar. "She doesn't know I'm here," he said. "I slipped the key from the ring before she left for work." The afternoon light was falling, and the light from the windows was green-blue. It would be dark soon. Carl didn't want to turn on a lamp. He couldn't tell if Michael had been drinking. Carl had been drinking some last night. He decided to sit at the kitchen table. He even considered opening his laptop, looking up results from other tracks.

Michael said, "I wanted to see if there was anything I left behind that I still wanted. I used to live here…for about five minutes. She said she didn't want me back in here, it was your place now. I can't have her telling me what to do all the time. Not just yet." Michael slouched low on the couch. He sat with his knees apart and turned to Carl when he said, "You do anything today?"

Carl held the bottle in his hand. His eyes were on the label. "No."

"She used you, man."

"So?"

A laugh came from Michael. "You must not care about anything. You jocks."

"I could've talked till I was blue in the face trying to explain what a tool you are, Michael."

Michael looked straight ahead again. "Yeah, well, maybe she should have listened to you. We're leaving, in a few days."

"Please don't tell me you are here looking for a tip on a horse," Carl said.

Michael said, "I just told you why I was here." There was nothing spoken between them for some time. The light inside the room changed, held some scarlet and gold. Michael said, "I've walked through this apartment three times already. I don't want anything from this place. But, I had to come here to find that out. You can understand that, can't you?"

"You have her back and now you don't want her?"

Michael's voice turned quieter when he said, "That's not what I'm saying at all."

"If I had one wish in the world right now it would be that you would simply evaporate."

"I know. I know. What's going to be different, jock? You seem to know a lot of things."

"I know horses."

"That's not what I am talking about." Michael pulled himself up from the loveseat. He sat forward, let his arms dangle between his knees. "What's different?"

"I'm not going to give you advice about your own wife."

Michael offered a dumb-looking grin. "You don't know, or you won't tell me?" The expression on his face seemed to be a mixture of defiance and defeat. He looked like he was about to say, *Unbelievable.* "I think I really came over here to see you," he said. "Tell you that we were leaving Cleveland. I think that you think I'm afraid of you. But I came over here to tell you I'm not."

"I should've told Christine how I felt about her right away. She wouldn't have let me live here, though." He wasn't talking to Michael, but Carl wanted to say these words out loud, in front of someone. "I would've been just another guy."

The men looked at one another for longer than a minute. Michael said, "She's never said anything bad about you."

Carl's eyes went to the window and they stayed there. "Goodbye, Michael."

The apartment had turned shadowy. From the corner of his eye, Carl saw Michael stand. Michael walked for the door quickly. When he closed the door it left a sharp sound in Carl's ears.

13.

Carl worked out the horses at Summit before returning to the apartment. The morning light was bright and he sat at the kitchen table and leafed through the pages of the *Racing Form* while he wore his reading glasses. He hadn't worn them when Christine was around. He'd known what he wanted to say; he hadn't needed to check past-performance lines. He studied the feature race for a time. Carl had a mount, McKenzie Bridge, a plodding long shot that seemed to be in over its head. But the thing was, the other horses in the race were all speed-burners. There came a sound at the front door, a key in the lock, the lock turning. The door opened and only then did she knock on it. "Anyone home?"

No. He said, "Over here." He took off his glasses, folded them in one hand. She wore clogs, pantyhose, a gray dress and windbreaker-type jacket with the collar turned up. She stood by the table with her hands in the pockets of the jacket. "Who's getting married?"

"We went to St. Paul's for mass," she said with a flap of both arms.

"You already got him going to church?"

"He's the Catholic. We're going to the races this afternoon. You going to live in the apartment? You gonna spy on Mrs. Lovain, ask her out?"

"She's old enough to be my mother."

"No, she isn't."

"Haven't really had time to think about whether I'll stay here, Christine. You said you had already paid..."

"We're going to pay," she said. "Haven't done it as yet. I'm still kind of organizing things."

Catholic Church, racetrack. It sounded like Michael was running things. Still, Christine was pretty good at the racetrack. Better than him.

"I wanted to bring over my key," she said. "Michael told me about yesterday."

"I'd have done the same thing."

"No, you wouldn't have."

"I was crazy, too," he said. "Back when." He tried to grin. "You leaving the chairs here? The table?"

"Michael has a table and chairs at his place. These are..."

"Imitations."

"Right."

Carl guided the empty chair back from the table. "Have a seat for a minute," he said. "He's outside right now, waiting?"

"I drove over here alone."

"His idea?"

She didn't respond.

Carl said, "So, you're not Catholic?"

"Not really."

"You know, one day I might be a churchgoing man myself. Please sit. I'll only beg you to stay for a while. Then, I have to get to the track."

Christine moved the chair closer and sat. She appeared to deflate. Her arms were limp at her sides. Her eyes went to the *Racing Form* spread out on the table and then over to Carl. "You going to start winning races again anytime soon?"

He said, "I hired an agent. On Thursday. Gary Shales."

"I don't know a Gary Shales. Doesn't hang out at the bar, does he?"

"Yeah, well. I think Gary just keeps to himself."

"You needed an agent," she said. "How come you never wanted one in the first place?"

They had talked about this before. He wanted to offer a different response. There were different truths to it. He didn't like the past-tense usage of need. Carl said, "I got used to the fact I wasn't going to have a great career. A great career means people do things for you. I learned how to do everything on my own."

"You don't want help?"

"I'd rather be the jockey who doesn't like agents rather than a jockey ditched by them."

"So why do you have one now?"

"Well, I just got back from California, didn't I?" He said this and then he cracked a smile, though maybe to her it didn't look like much of one. He said, "I talk to each of my ex-wives every year at Christmas. Stay around for a while and I'll add you to the list." Christine crossed her arms. He wanted to injure them both a bit, but she didn't appear to be interested. She looked to the front door, her eyes were focused on it. He said, "I just wanted to be someone different for a little while. That's what I like about being with you. It wouldn't have been forever anyway." She didn't look in his direction. "I don't know what that says about the life I was leading beforehand. Other than it was bullshit."

She said, "You don't believe that."

Neither of them spoke for a time. Christine held a keychain in her right hand. Her fingers circled around it. He wasn't going to say the next thing.

"Carl," she said. She didn't want to say anything at all, he thought. She did turn to him partway and then her eyes went again to the *Form* on the table.

"Already?" he said. He wanted her to clear out then. He wanted to say, You can't do this. You do this and I will grow to hate you. There was no way he would talk with her about today's races. She had left him for another man a week ago. She was in love with her ex-husband. She had been a kind woman and now she was not.

Carl said, "What I really liked about having you around was that I was pretty sure I wasn't going to let you down. That is a very good feeling, Christine." He wanted her to look in his direction and when she did, he didn't speak. Her expression told him everything. Carl pointed to the *Form*. "I wouldn't tell you the horse I'm on in the feature is a sure thing today. Because I could never be sure of such a thing. But I keep looking at the race. It keeps making more sense to me. I see how it might go. I'd never make you a promise, though. I'd only tell you what I knew for certain. You know that." He swallowed. "But I don't want to talk about races with you anymore, all right?" He decided to turn a page of the *Form*. He put on his glasses. "Do you understand?"

"Yes." But what she said could barely be heard. She reached her hand over to the table and laid the keys there.

"Don't come back here," he said, as she walked for the door. There was nothing to it. No energy, no emphasis on any particular word. She closed the door and his eyes went back to the opened page of the *Racing Form*.

Carl won with two of his first four mounts that afternoon. In the feature, he gave a shrewd ride to McKenzie Bridge. They stayed on the rail for most of the trip and in the final hundred yards, the three horses remaining in front of him wilted. Carl swung McKenzie Bridge off the rail, weaved his way between the faders, intentionally brushed Hoyer on the number 4, though it wasn't enough to stop Hoyer from riding. Hoyer yelled after him, "Payback's comin', old dick!" McKenzie Bridge went on to win by two lengths at odds of 14–1. Carl sat atop McKenzie Bridge for the winner's circle photo, the horse breathing so hard Carl thought it might just take one more huge breath and then fall over dead. After weighing out and offering the saddle to a valet, Carl walked in a steady way for the jocks' room. He walked slow enough so that Christine might find him. He had one more horse to ride and Carl's insides seemed to be made of feathers. He had clued Christine in that things might turn out this way, but only when he'd said it to her had he felt he had a good chance.

Carl walked to the jockeys' room alone. His mount in the nightcap was a first-time starter, Bubble Wrap, trained by an Ian Willingham, a young British kid with a bad temper. His horses were all this way, too, but when a mean horse learned how to win, it could become a victory machine, especially in the bush leagues. Gary Shales had been a bit worried about this one, but underneath his indifferent demeanor, Gary might have been something of a fusspot, a worrywart. Carl didn't know him well enough yet. In the post parade, Bubble Wrap seemed tense and unhappy, and as she warmed up, she seemed to be holding her breath. Carl talked to her a bit, said he understood. "We're about to have a lot of fun together," he said to her at one point. In the starting gate, without any warning sign at all, she flipped. Carl was catapulted into the air. He landed on the point of his right shoulder. His face smashed into the dirt. He heard the sound of the horse grunt and wheeze and then it sprang onto its feet. There were hoofbeats, two sets of them, the filly running away and an outrider chasing her, and the hoofbeats faded. He was told later that when he was able to stand, he began to run from one outrider to the next, begging someone to push his shoulder back into place. Carl remembered nothing of this. He rode in an ambulance to Good Sam. He wanted to stay awake while his shoulder was set back in place, but the pain was too much. He had to be sedated. His treatment room had a television set and when he awakened, he watched an episode of Real Housewives of New Jersey. There was not a remote to be found. When the attending doctor appeared, he said, "You have a concussion. You need to stay with us overnight."

Gary Shales gave Carl a ride home from the hospital the next morning. He drove a Ford Celebrity, an early-model car that seemed to be in incredibly good condition. Gary said, "So."

Carl said, "Doc said it'll be a month before I'm ready to lift anything heavier than an inkpen."

"Need an operation?"

"He said I ought to think about it. Some ligament damage. It'll heal okay. Always does."

"Unbroke horses."

Carl raised his left hand to his mouth and coughed a weak-sounding cough. "I should've seen it coming. Some things I don't worry about. Just a part of me that isn't there."

Gary said, "What makes you a rider."

"Yeah. But then when you don't ride what do you have? You watch other people do it. You wonder."

Gary didn't need to answer and they rode along in silence. When he spoke he said, "Make money on other people doing it."

"Right. No offense."

"None taken."

"What are you going to do?"

"Have to look for somebody else. Wind up with somebody who doesn't know anything at all."

Carl wanted to laugh but his chest was weak. "Those guys can hit it big." Carl pointed, "Then just take a right up here."

Gary nodded. "They disappear, too."

"I know they do. That's the building, just pull to the curb."

Gary stopped the car and let out a breath. He gave a nod to Carl. "Need any help?"

"No," Carl said.

"Don't rush it."

"Right." He reached for the handle to open the door. Gary got out, walked around the front of the car. "I got it," Carl said, though he was by himself inside the car. Gary arrived at his side, opened the passenger door. Carl pulled himself out of there. "Bye," Carl said. "Thanks."

"Liked working with you," Gary said. "Short time we had."

"Yep."

14.

They gave him a prescription of forty Percodan tablets and even though Carl could feel the pills darken his mood every day, he went through them like breath mints. He took the pills and though he couldn't feel pain in his shoulder, he began to obsess over the notion that he would never feel strong again. Every day, he brooded. He imagined that one day—and perhaps this day would arrive sooner than he had ever imagined—his days would be filled with nothing but pain. This would happen because he had chosen the life he had. He had been injured in some way every year of his career. Many of the injuries were the kind he could ride right through. When Carl had been laid up before, he would have vague thoughts about the future, a time in his life when there would be no more riding. If you were a rider and then you were no longer a rider, what would you think about if there wasn't the next race to think about? Maybe you could do the next best thing, just try to stay around racing in some way. But there would be the longing, the acknowledgment of all that was now over for good. What would your mind be able to overcome? Carl supposed that when the time arrived, perhaps he would just have to leave the racetrack forever. There was another world out there, of course he was aware of this. People always said this, especially when a life they were used to was about to shut down. It was talk, stupid talk, brave talk. The only life that meant anything was the one you felt you had to lead. This was the life that didn't make all the sense in the world. The life where you didn't have all the facts. When Carl was a younger rider and just struggling to survive, he didn't care about twenty or forty years in the future. Either he would be a man who hit the jackpot or he would be a man who didn't. If he didn't, then so be it. Anyway, he'd never believed that wouldn't be him. His heart and his hands were strong. As long as he was not injured beyond repair, the man who didn't hit the jackpot would never be him. He wasn't injured badly now; a separated shoulder would heal. The ache would go on for a year, maybe he would feel it on and off for a long time. One day soon enough he would be able to guide the reins, bring the whip back.

The check from Tom Westfeld's office arrived in the mail a few days after Carl injured his shoulder. There had been a deduction for Christine's first-class ticket. A typed note on Amarillo Holding Ltd. stationery explained this. Carl thought, I gave this woman too much. At another time in his life, the check from Westfeld would have seemed like a lot of money. Now Carl had a check and a bank book and the apartment he wanted for the spring and summer. All of this would get him to the next place, the next town, when it was time for that. If he were twenty years younger, Westfeld's check would have hit him in a different way. He understood as much, and it scared him.

One night, he lost track of how many Percodan he took. He went to shake another from the vial but the vial was empty. His body went cold. His right arm was in a sling and he touched at his right hand with his left. He brought his left hand to his face. It was as if he were standing outside in the middle of Manitoba on a January night. He began to tremble. He needed to find the bathroom; it felt as if he were screaming. His computer was there and he needed to write a note. He typed with one hand.

Carl passed out and when he awakened, he was under a plastic chair. He was looking up at the seat. Carl turned to his side and began to vomit. He crawled into the bathroom and once he finished heaving his guts into the toilet, he peeled off his clothes with his good hand and lay down in the bathtub and worked the hot- and cold-water spigots with his feet. He filled the tub to his shoulders and lay still until the water became cool. When he decided to climb out from the bathtub, he reached for the metallic soap dish with his left hand. Water ran down his sides as he walked for the bedroom. Under the covers of the bed, his bones felt like scrap metal. He wanted someone to slip into bed and hold him, a large woman. He wanted her to put her arms around him and say, My beautiful, beautiful boy. He lay curled up in bed and he thought about this for a long time. He didn't fall asleep. He was not hungry, and he was not thirsty.

Once Carl was able to sit up in bed, he had to hold himself in place by bending his knees and leaning his shoulders forward. His forehead rested on the space of blanket between his knees. He felt better and worse now. His behavior had been histrionic, but it also had been necessary. The way he'd felt lying in bed, shaking cold and wet, it was as if he were about to morph into another creature altogether. He'd been on the verge of complete surrender. Nothing had happened. He remained the same. No one had come for him. No one had seen what he had done, how he had acted. He laid his forehead on the space of blanket between his knees and he tried to imagine what Christine might have said if she had seen him behave this way. Michael, Carl thought—there's a guy who has had some moments. Carl wanted to laugh, but not in a cruel way. Suddenly he thought of Christine at age fifty and he felt his heart sicken.

Christine was a young woman, but she probably understood some things about men. If she were still here, she might've understood what Carl was going through. Carl lifted his head and looked around the room. He drooled a bit and wiped his mouth with the back of his hand. Still nude, he walked out into the living room. It smelled of rotting fish. He cleaned the floor with liquid dish soap and paper towels and he found Lemon Pledge under the sink and sprayed it in the air over where the trail of vomit had been. He sat down at the kitchen table and took deep breaths. His sling was draped over the back of the chair and he leaned forward and reached his left hand around to fetch it. He slipped on the sling and then looked to his darkened computer screen. He recalled sitting here the night before. He tapped the space bar and the screen lightened. In a Word document he'd typed,

what happend to

He couldn't remember at all the direction this might have been going in. He moved the mouse and the arrow went to the top right-hand corner of the screen. He clicked on the red square with the white X and the computer asked if he wanted to save it. He clicked No.

The apartment hadn't been cleaned since Christine moved out. He prepared to do this—brought out a bucket, liquid soap, a scrub brush—and wondered if and when he might see her again. He wondered if and when he would see the other women who had never really left his imagination. He thought of them as a group, gathered in the room. They would look at him on his knees, a bucket at his side, a scrub brush in his free hand. You didn't see this coming, Carl? one voice would finally say. He would say, I did, I did, and not look up.

Carl spent some of the morning working on the floors. Leaning forward caused his hurt shoulder to throb and periodically he had to stop. Before, she had done it. He would arrive home from the races in the afternoon and could tell she had mopped up. She didn't clean the floors on any kind of schedule and he wondered what had prompted her to clean the floors when she did. Footprints from the cat. Shoe prints, his. Perhaps her own. Perhaps someone else's. It was always so sloppy outside. He thought of her returning here after making her bets and sitting up in bed with her laptop, Michael laid out alongside her. They waited for the results to come in. Carl surveyed the floors and he thought a man looked at a woman as something of a fool and vice versa because one person always understood one thing the other could never seem to. There was the additional need in everyone to stop making sense of everything. So, couples were going to hit a dead end. Carl supposed that if he had to identify what he was a fool for, he would not say it was Christine. Not for certain. This time, that prize might not go to a woman. He finished the floor in the living room, then decided to sit on the loveseat and watch it dry. Because of Big Zip, Carl had believed he could have a life like this. He had to try; no one could fault him for that. His ride on Big Zip in the San Diego Handicap was nothing but a study in fear. Things had not gone well there. Things didn't go well in general. He wanted to talk with someone about this right now. He wanted to know about the ride he had given the horse. No one here brought it up. It was a last-place finish, what else needed to be said? Carl stepped across the damp floor, walked flat-footed across it to the kitchen table, and sat down. He opened his phone and clicked through the numbers. He wanted to call Tom Westfeld and ask him about the ride. Westfeld was as high up as they got. Westfeld wouldn't have applauded Carl's ride, and Carl understood this. Westfeld probably felt foolish about the entire Big Zip experiment. But he also might confirm the fact that Carl had done as best he could. Carl found the number and clicked the dial button and the phone rang once on the other end before Carl decided to hang up. It seemed wrong. It seemed weak. At best, Carl understood Westfeld would simply patronize him. If Westfeld would even bother to talk to him at all. It felt terrible to seek this type of forgiveness. Carl understood he was simply off his game right now. He wasn't riding regularly. He needed to sober up and stay smart. But where to go from here, he was not as certain about that. He opened his phone again and found a California number he wanted. He dialed, waited. Out there, it would be late morning, right after training hours. On the third ring, there was an answer. He heard the voice and Carl said, "Tab, this is Carl Arvo calling from Cleveland."

"Carl Arvo," Tab's voice said. "Didn't think I'd hear from you again."

Carl decided to ignore the implications of this remark. He said, "How's it going out there? Got anything running today?"

"Yeah, got one."

"Gonna win?" Carl hoped it sounded as if he were just being polite. He didn't feel as desperate, not like earlier today.

"Yeah," Tab said. "It will."

"You serious?"

After a pause, Tab said, "Always. Look, you're calling…for a tip?"

"No." There came a pause. How could it not have been obvious? Carl said, "I wanted to know about Big Zip. I wanted to know how he was doing. I wanted to check up on—"

"He's been sold," Tab said. "To some outfit in Arizona. He left for Turf Paradise a couple of days ago, actually."

"Sold him, huh?"

"Either that or they were going to run him in a claiming race here. We paid a half mil for him, it would look like a fire sale. Boss doesn't want that. That horse is someone else's headache now. You wanted to see if you could ride him again?"

"I'm laid up," Carl said. "Separated my shoulder last week." Tab didn't respond. "You guys got a good barn out there, Tab. I'm glad I got to see something like it."

"Sure."

"Arizona, huh? Turf Paradise? Shit, he'll be a king there."

"Maybe. Look, is there anything else I can for you?"

"No," Carl said, right away. "Maybe I'll see you around, Tab."

"Sure thing."

Carl closed his phone and set it on the table. He crossed his legs and pictured a map of America, one where the states were all different colors. He thought of Arizona, the shape of the state, how and where it fit on the map. Someone out there was using their head. The tracks out there were dry and fast and they played to speed. The purses were half of what they offered at places like Balboa, and the level of competition reflected this. Carl had never been to Arizona, had never ridden at Turf Paradise, and he tried to picture Big Zip out there, racing in front. It was a pretty sight. The sunlight glinted on the horse's shoulders and neck as it made for the far turn with a daylight lead. If he was looked after the right way, Big Zip could be a good horse there.

Carl felt light-headed and queasy, but it was an improvement. He sat quietly in the modern ghost chair at the kitchen table and dipped his head. He felt himself breathe. His shoulder burned. He began to feel everything.

What had Tab said about a horse running today that was going to win? Carl had asked, just wanted to sound interested, and Tab had said what he had said. Carl tried to figure out what this really meant. Tab was on cruise control, he wasn't any horse player. But he paid attention and in his own way he seemed pretty smart. He worked for a wealthy man's stable and he did what he was told. Everything he had said had been right on. Because the horse was trained by Henry Forrest, it probably wouldn't be much of a price. The races wouldn't begin out there for a couple more hours, so Carl had time to sort it out. Somewhere in this apartment he had that uncashed check from Tom Westfeld. He had the savings account Christine had started for him. Of course, he couldn't bet all of this money on the single word of someone. But Carl might go a thousand dollars. Carl hadn't made a bet on anything since he'd gone to California.

He thought of Christine. He supposed he couldn't help himself. He was living in an apartment that had once been theirs, but she wasn't coming back—not with him and his bum shoulder waiting for her. He hadn't spoken with her since the day he had injured his shoulder. Carl had ridden three winners that day. If he dialed her up right now, she might answer. No matter where she was or if Michael was with her. He keyed in her number himself and then pressed dial. The phone rang three times and he knew it would go to voicemail, but then there was her voice on the other end and she said, "Hello there, Carl." She was outside.

"Sounds like you are in the car," he said.

"I am."

"I didn't think I would catch you. I was going to leave a message."

"Yeah? What's going on?"

"I was talking to…where are you? It doesn't sound like you're here."

"We're driving through South Dakota now, of all places."

Carl waited. He didn't want to say anything else. "South Dakota."

"We're driving through the lower section of this state, I think." She said something he didn't catch. "Man, there is nothing out here." It seemed as if Michael spoke then, a few lines of gibberish, and Christine said, "Oh, shut the fuck up," in a nice-enough way.

"When did this happen?" Carl said.

"What?" she said. "I saw you get hurt. I called the jocks' room, they gave me the prognosis. You okay?"

"Sure," he said. "I needed a break."

"I don't like summer in the Midwest. Never have, if I am being honest about it."

"No," he said, though he didn't know what to make of this. What's in South Dakota? he thought. He supposed this was not their final destination.

"I was going to call you," she said.

"That's all right."

"So what's happening? What was that?" she said.

"Are there any OTBs out where you are? I got a horse for you. Runs in a couple of hours, I think."

In a moment, she said, "Oh, please. You don't have to keep doing this." Carl couldn't decide how much she wanted Michael to know. He tried to picture them on a highway, out in the middle of a vacant plain. Somewhere farther away would be rolling mountains, infinite pines.

He said, "Atokad Park is in one of the Dakotas. That's Dakota spelled backwards."

"Oh, I know," she said. "Listen, we paid our rent for the rest of the lease…hey, just drive, all right?" she said.

"Oh, great."

"Carl," she said.

"I got this on the word from somebody who doesn't play the horses," Carl said. "That's why I think it's a solid play. I wouldn't have called you otherwise."

She didn't speak for a moment and the line seemed muffled. "Carl?" she said, after some time.

"Yes?"

"We're not stopping until we get to Oregon. Oregon or bust for the summer. Fuck the holy grind! See the USA, man."

"They run short meets up in the Dakotas. Maybe a month long. Then you have to move on to someplace else." Carl said. "Otherwise I might have tried one when I was younger. Can't get established in a short time, though. Obviously, they don't run in the winter."

"You sure?" she said.

"No," he said. "I'm not sure actually."

"Take care of yourself. I'll be looking for you when we make it to the simulcast parlors."

"I'll be there," he said. "I'll be the guy in front early."

"That's where we'll look!"

Carl closed his phone fast, placed it on the table. This day, he thought. Then he decided he didn't want to think about what had happened so far. What he wanted more than anything was to understand whether or not this day could still hold some luck for him. He had been alone but it seemed as if a lot had happened. What he tried to do now was not think of anything specific, he just tried to focus on how everything all together felt. He wanted to understand everything and then he wanted to work on not feeling as if he needed to. He sat at the table for a while. He would arrive at a point he had invariably found in the past. And the point was that he was tough and he always got past what he couldn't change. He tried to feel fortunate.

Finally, he thought, Now where did I put that goddamn check?

15.

Later, Carl drove over to his bank, then the simulcast parlor at Summit Park. The live races were going on, though he wasn't interested in any of that now. He knew the hostess at the simulcast parlor—Lottie or Tottie—and when she pointed to his injured arm, he turned his hand in the sling, gave her a thumbs-up. He paid a buck twenty-five for a Balboa program and stood beyond the last row of cubicles that faced the wall of TV sets. He found the Henry Forrest–trained horse in the seventh race, a three-year-old filly owned by Tom Westfeld, Golden Beebee. Odds of 5–2 on the morning line. Carl walked over to a betting window and put a thousand dollars on it to win.

He drove back to the apartment and checked the race results on his computer. Golden Bebee won her race easily and paid off at final odds of 7–5. The stretch runs of all the Balboa races were available on the track's website and Carl watched the seventh after he found out about the results. It was sunny out there and Westfeld's green-and-gold colors were far ahead of the others. The filly had been bet heavily. It was no secret. His shoulder ached and Carl was out of pills and he understood that he wasn't going to take any more.

The morning after this—each morning after this—he awakened before five a.m., made coffee, then drove to L.A. Fitness over on Superior Avenue. He put on his headphones, listened to the local college rock station. He didn't know any of the songs at all and while he listened, he worked out on a treadmill or a Stairmaster or an elliptical machine. His body was tired and he was no longer surprised by how much everything hurt. He was recovering. He put away the sling. He kept to himself. One day, just to make things a little more interesting, he tried to go an entire day without speaking. He made it until around four in the afternoon and then his cell rang and when it did, the number was not from his area code. He decided to answer. He said, "Hello." The person on the other end was looking for Mario. "Sorry," Carl said. After he hung up, he said, "Son of a bitch."

He felt blue, but he understood that he had reason to. One day, Gary Shales called. They greeted each other and then Gary waited. He said, "I'm gonna go up and see Lori."

"She's where again?" Carl said.

"Heading for Canterbury right now."

"Minnesota."

"Right."

"What are you going to do, Gary?"

"I want to check up on her. She needs representation."

"She a better rider than me?"

Gary laughed. "Right now, yeah."

Carl said, "Hell, I think we would have done all right together, you and me."

Gary spoke slowly. "I know it."

"Minnesota is probably a nice place," Carl said. "I've heard good things."

"Summer's best time to be there."

Carl said, "Okay, man."

"Bye."

Carl worked out at L.A. Fitness every day and he showered there, then returned to the apartment for a quick snack and an hour of checking on horse-racing news from all across the country. He'd click open a string of websites, then look over future entries for the tracks in his region: Charles Town, Penn National, Mountaineer, Great Lakes, Steel Meadows. He looked for the names of the horses he had ridden and who was named to ride them now. He still felt a connection to Balboa Park and was interested in the entries there. He'd check the entries for Turf Paradise in Phoenix, then would head for the bedroom and take a nap.

In the evenings he sat at the kitchen table and periodically looked over to Mrs. Lovain's apartment. Her life seemed steady. She didn't have any men over there with her. She would look over from time to time, see that Carl was watching. Once she gave him an odd look and when she did he felt humiliated. This was always the downside to voyeurism. The way people worked on their lives was a private thing. They should be able to do this with their blinds opened or closed. Carl simply wanted to know how his life stacked up. He didn't need nor did he desire to see people in the nude. If they were that way, he would watch. He would watch otherwise, when there was a chance to. At the racetrack, he had plenty of numbers and statistics to go by. Otherwise, he did not. When he watched others through their windows, he was thrilled with the imperfection there, all that could not be tabulated. It always told him just enough. When Mrs. Lovain spotted him, something in Carl fell. He lifted his window and stuck himself partway through the opening. He waved to her and continued to wave until she opened her kitchen window. He held one hand to the side of his mouth. "I'm Carl," he said.

"I know," she said.

"Oh." He set both hands at the bottom of the window sill and looked up and down the alley. A dumpster was at one end, the street the other. He looked in her direction again. "Christine left. I guess you know that."

The woman nodded.

He thought about saying, Got back with her ex. One of the things he knew about Mrs. Lovain was that she had an ex. He said, "She understood everything."

Mrs. Lovain didn't react. She wore reading glasses. Carl waved to her. Mrs. Lovain waved back, closed her window. They returned to their kitchen tables.

Near the end of May, he saw Big Zip's name in the entries at Turf Paradise and when this happened, a feeling came over him that he had not been expecting. He saw the words and it was as if he had seen his own name. It was a strange feeling. Part of him was out there, part of him still hadn't found its place. He booked a flight for Phoenix, for the day of the race. He checked on the price of first class and decided to fly coach.

On the day of the race, Carl flew out to Phoenix on an American Airlines 737 jet. He sat between an older black man and a middle-aged white man. Carl paid three dollars for headphones and watched the movie, something with Jennifer Aniston. The men on either side of him slept. At the Phoenix airport, Carl hailed a taxi and when he arrived at Turf Paradise, there were still three hours before post time of Big Zip's race. He sat in the open-air grandstand, stuck on his reading glasses and looked over a West Coast edition of the *Racing Form.* He held the *Form* with both hands and studied the horses in Big Zip's race. He spotted his name there, Arvo, C., on the running line for Big Zip's San Diego Handicap. It seemed strange, out of place, in the same column as the other great jockeys who had been given rides on the horse. When he looked up from the *Form*, his eyes went out to the racetrack and he felt lightheaded. He thought, Good lord, what am I doing out here? Where am I? He thought, What have I done with my life? He knew, of course. Inside, deep down, he knew exactly. It was a Friday afternoon, early in the day, and the stands were nearly vacant. Carl steadied himself. People had thoughts like this every day. Carl murmured to himself. He said, "I know where I am." His eyes went to the *Form* again. Big Zip was the class of this bunch. Carl expected him to win handily.

When it was time for Big Zip's race, Carl thought about walking down to the paddock area, seeing the horse up close. He decided to stay where he was. On the track for the post parade, Big Zip seemed a trifle heavy. The horse had been raced steadily by Henry Forrest and perhaps the new trainer decided to take it easy. This time it probably wouldn't matter. The runners assembled to race against Big Zip—on paper anyway—couldn't seem to get out of their own way. Someone named Roger Powell had the riding assignment on Big Zip.

After the break, Big Zip darted smartly to the front and Powell let the horse roll for the first furlong. They opened up a three-length lead and then the jock reined him in a bit, tried to save something for the stretch. It was a competent technique, though if you knew Big Zip, you knew the best way was to just cut it loose, let it go as fast as it could for as long as it could. The horse turned in to the homestretch with a big lead but began to tire with a furlong left and one runner came bursting free from the back of the pack and almost caught them at the finish. Carl hadn't bet the race, he hadn't wanted to jinx anything, and he was glad to see Big Zip hang on for victory. Carl thought about sneaking down and getting in the winner's circle photo, but a moment later thought better of that, too. He didn't need a memento. He didn't need proof that he had been here. He wouldn't forget it. He let his eyes find the infield toteboard. Carl needed to leave soon, catch his flight back to Cleveland.

Big Zip should have won the race by daylight, and the trainer, if he was any kind of trainer at all, would understand the horse would need to be cranked up tighter for its next start. The race was done and the horses that had run in it were being walked up the homestretch. Beyond the oval, palm trees dotted the stable area. It's very quiet here, he thought. This trip had not been a flight of fancy. He'd wanted to see that Big Zip had some good racing left in him. Carl wanted to see him racing in the western sunshine, and he wanted to see Big Zip win. He belongs here, Carl thought. It seemed to be an important thing to acknowledge, even if Carl could have just watched the race from the simulcast parlor at Summit and wound up understanding the same thing. Carl didn't know how he would have felt if he had done that, however. This had been the way to go. Fly out here, watch the race, see things exactly. He wanted to see the horse race on the lead early, that had been the best part. That was all he wanted to think about now. He sat in the stands and let his eyes fall on all that was before him. He had that long. He would not miss his flight back.